A LEANER MEANER MIDLIFE

GOOD TO THE LAST DEATH

BOOK 11

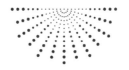

ROBYN PETERMAN

JOIN MY NEWSLETTER!

ACKNOWLEDGMENTS

The Good To The Last Death Series is a pleasure to write. A Leaner Meaner Midlife was a joy and an obsession for me. Telling stories is my passion and my passion has been fulfilled with this series. Daisy, Gideon and the gang bring me an absurd amount of joy and I hope you feel the same way. See some old friends and meet some new ones!

As always, writing may be a solitary sport, but it takes a whole bunch of people to make the magic happen.

Renee — Thank you for my beautiful cover and for being the best badass critique partner in the world. TMB. LOL

Wanda — You are the freaking bomb. Love you to the moon and back.

Heather, Nancy, Caroline, Susan and Wanda — Thank you for reading early and helping me find the booboos. You all rock.

My Readers — Thank you for loving the stories that come from my warped mind. It thrills me.

Steve, Henry and Audrey — Your love and support makes all of this so much more fun. I love you people endlessly.

DEDICATION

For Wanda—the furry one and the not furry one. I love you both.

MORE IN THE GOOD TO THE LAST DEATH SERIES

ORDER BOOK 12 TODAY!

BOOK DESCRIPTION

A LEANER MEANER MIDLIFE

I want to live my life in peace for a little while as opposed to pieces. I don't know who I have to bribe to catch a break, but I'm willing to pay the big bucks.

Apparently, no one got the memo. Midlife is one messy ride.

Fine. I'm off to Lexington, Kentucky to find a self-proclaimed dragon who sports a mullet, beer belly and delusions of Immortal grandeur. This time he's gone too far. He's messed with me and mine for the last time.

The way to end a dragon is to remove his tail. We thought we had. A tail is in the back. Right?

Wrong.

So, so wrong.

With the love of my Immortal life by my side along with a few smack-talking, geriatric Nephilim and a foul-mouthed, tooth-pick loving Keeper of Fate, I'm ready.

And when it's done, I'm taking a freaking vacation. I've earned it.

It's time to slay the dragon for good.

This time there will be no mercy.

CHAPTER ONE

MICK JAGGER WAS CORRECT. YOU CAN'T ALWAYS GET WHAT YOU want. I just prayed we would eventually get what we needed. The permanent end of Micky Muggles was on the top of the list.

The transport home after the battle had been as bad as the trip to the parallel plane where the battle had taken place. The nutty Nephilim, Jolly Sue, had spoken the words of the spell to leave, and no one, except the Keeper of Fate, had come through it unscathed. Lura Belle walloped her sister in the head upon arrival back home. She called Jolly Sue a spleeny, unmuzzled horn-beast and insisted that the next time we plane jumped, she would be the one to chant the spell. She claimed she was a better travel guide and wouldn't let her guests feel like they were being burned alive.

There would be no *next time* as far as I was concerned. That chapter was closed... I hoped.

Dimple, kooky sibling to Jolly Sue and Lura Belle, had puked in the kitchen sink. Zander and his sister, Catriona, went up to our guest rooms to sleep off the horrific journey.

My siblings, Prue, Abby and Rafe followed after our new guests to make sure they were comfortable. The ever-fabulous and always disgusting Candy Vargo chuckled as she watched Zander try to hold Prue's hand as they departed. It was a developing story, and I had high hopes for a happy ending attached to it. We could all use one of those.

Tory looked exhausted. She'd expended too much magic for the benefit of her worst enemy—the *finally* gone forever Zadkiel. I knew she would live with no regrets. She'd said what she wanted to the man who had hurt her beyond comprehension, and she'd given those she cared for the chance to do the same. Gabe hovered over her even though she kept weakly slapping him away.

My brother didn't give up easily. He wore his heart on his sleeve and didn't have any intention of hiding his feelings. They'd been separated for a thousand years due to Zadkiel's psychotic lies. My guess was that if it took a thousand more to win her back, Gabe would gladly do it.

What I wanted now was to live my life in peace for a little while as opposed to pieces. I didn't know who I had to bribe to catch a break, but I was willing to pay the big bucks.

I couldn't believe it was only eight in the morning. It felt as if we'd been gone for a year, but it had only been a little over twelve hours. None of us had gotten any sleep. I was tired, but wired. Sleep would come soon enough. I needed to bask in the glow of love and friends first. We'd briefed everyone about Zadkiel's end. As expected, no one shed a tear. The Micky Muggles discussion, along with his departing threat to return, would happen after some coffee.

The house was filled with people I loved. Most importantly, Alana Catherine was on her way home with our friends who'd protected her while Gideon and I couldn't. My gratitude for them was immense. The safe word, *toothpick*, had been shared with everyone and we were as secure as we could be at the moment. The thought of holding my baby in my arms again and breastfeeding her made me giddy. Her milk-drunk expression of love was necessary for me to feel whole. Gideon had barely let me out of his sight since we'd arrived. He'd opened the front door so many times to check on Alana Catherine's impending arrival that the room was freezing. Charlie just laughed and made a roaring fire in the stone fireplace. The crackle and dancing of the flickering flames were hypnotic.

"Darlings!" Dirk squealed as he strutted into the living room like it was his own personal catwalk. The fabulous queen, aka one of the Four Horsemen of the Apocalypse, wore a bright orange sequined ballgown trimmed in marabou. It would have been a hideous eyesore on anyone else. Dirk made it work. "Wonderful news! In celebration of Zadkiel's demise, Tim has prepared a breakfast casserole called Turkey-Noodle-Dooda-Surprise hotdish. Smells divine."

"Debatable," Gideon whispered.

I agreed. "Wait. What does Turkey-Noodle-haha have to do with Zadkiel?"

"It's Turkey-Noodle-Dooda-Surprise hotdish," Dirk corrected me. "And I don't know how it connects to the dead bastard, but our Tim is brilliant and works in mysterious ways. I just love our adorable, somewhat socially inept Immortal!"

"Is there actually turkey in it?" Heather asked with a small gag as she placed a cool washcloth on Dimple's head and got her comfortable in the overstuffed armchair.

"I have no idea," Dirk admitted with a giggle. "There were so many ingredients I couldn't tell you. But I did notice he used hot sauce and jelly. Simply the best!"

Best wasn't the word I'd use. Inedible was more accurate.

Thankfully, turkey-doodle-dodo wasn't in my future. Being a vegetarian rocked.

Heather sat down next to me and leaned close. "I'll go to the Piggly Wiggly in a bit and get something edible."

"Donuts," I whispered. "Glazed."

My sister gave me a thumbs up. "Your wish is my command."

"Turkey-Noodle-Hooha sounds tasty," Candy Vargo said dropping down onto the couch and putting her feet on the coffee table. "I think we need to discuss the fuckin' fucker. Micky Muggle's is a hemorrhoid on the ass of humanity."

I didn't have the energy to yell at her or knock her feet off the furniture. It also seemed unimportant to clarify that *hooha* was a nickname for a vagina. The coffee was helping, but there was only so much I could handle on so little sleep.

"Do we have to do it right this minute?" I asked, cuddling up to Gideon on the other couch. "I just want one second to enjoy no one I love being in mortal danger."

I looked up at Gideon's gorgeous face and a smile tugged at the corner of my lips. His eyes were glued to the front door. His anticipation of our daughter coming home made me love the man even more than I already did.

"One question, please," Heather said. "Is Micky Muggles alive or dead?"

"Unclear," Gabe replied. "The gals bit his ass off, so the consensus is that once the rest of the magic fades, he'll revert to true age and die since he has nowhere to store the magic."

"Come again?" Charlie asked, confused. "Did you actually say they *bit* his ass off?"

"Damn straight," Jolly Sue stated with a gag. "Went for the tail like Candy Vargo commanded. It was nasty and the taste wasn't good, but we got the job done."

"Fuckin' gnarly," Candy announced, grinning at the Nephilim. "My gals have big lady-balls and outstandin' chompers."

"The toothpicks were a godsend," Lura Belle commented. "Biting an ass off is more complicated than it sounds. And having ass stuck between your teeth is quite unpleasant."

"In all my centuries I've never heard of anything like this," Charlie muttered, going a little green. "I suppose I was expecting the use of a sword for the removal of the tail... umm... ass."

"A sword would have been a heck of a lot less bloody," Dimple acknowledged. "I still have the taste of metal in my mouth. I'm hopin' the Turkey-Noodle-Dooda-Surprise will take it away."

"Oh shit," I said, getting to my feet. "Did you gals swallow any of his blood? Did you feel any kind of rush?"

Lura Belle wrinkled her brow in thought. "Well, yes. I assumed the rush came from biting an ass off of a person. I've never done that before."

"And I never want to do it again," Dimple choked out, holding her stomach and scurrying to the bathroom.

I was glad she was going to aim for the toilet this time instead of the kitchen sink. Her loud retching made my gag reflex kick in.

"Poor old gal," Dirk said, following her to help out.

"Is the rush an issue?" Gideon asked.

"Possibly," I answered. Lura Belle and Jolly Sue were sprawled out on the loveseat. I eyed them warily. "If you swallowed some of his blood, you might have some of his power."

"Oh! Hell's bells," Dimple screeched from the half-bath by the kitchen right before she emptied the contents of her stomach for the third time.

9

Jolly Sue shook her head and groaned. "I don't want more power. Just got rid of the awful gift I've been stuck with since I was born."

Lura Belle was appalled at the news. "How long will it last?"

"How much do you think you ingested?" I asked.

"Not much," she replied with a shudder of disgust. "I got more on me than in me. Does flesh count as blood because I might have swallowed a section of the butt."

If someone had told me that I'd be talking to a hundred-and-something-year-old woman about the finer points of biting off an ass and whether swallowing some of it was a bad thing, I would have punched them in the head. Right now, I would happily punch myself in the head not to have this conversation.

"Candy, can you field that question?" I asked. She'd kind of been there and done that when she'd eaten Gabe, Prue, Abby and Rafe all those years ago.

We were hitting all the gag-inducing subjects this morning. I might be joining Dimple in the bathroom shortly.

"Sure," she said, taking the toothpick out of her mouth and tucking it behind her ear. "I'm gonna go with a no on the butt flesh question unless you ate an artery."

"Jesus," Gideon muttered, pressing the bridge of his nose.

"Hey, Tim," Candy yelled. "I need some expert advice."

Tim hustled into the living room from the kitchen, where he'd been hard at work creating something that smelled really bad. He wore one of my aprons over his mail uniform. "How can I be of service, friend?"

"Does an ass have arteries?" she asked.

Tim thought for a moment, then pulled out the ever-present notebook from one of his many pockets. "Luckily, I've studied the buttock recently. I was searching for a gross fact that might surprise Jennifer and make her laugh." He flipped through the pages. "Ah, here we go. The inferior gluteal artery is in the buttock, and it supplies oxygenated blood to the glute muscles. So yes, there's an artery."

"Thanks," Candy said.

Tim wasn't done. "And while we're on the subject of butts… a hairy butt actually serves a purpose."

"I'd like to stop you right there," Tory said with a groan.

Tim giggled. "Can you live without knowing why a hirsute bum is a good thing?"

Tory squinted at him and tried not to smile. She failed. It was good to see her happy or, at least, not completely miserable. Gross facts for the win.

"Fine," she conceded. "Tell me about furry rumps. I'm quite sure I'll live to regret asking."

"Very well then," Tim said with a naughty twinkle in his eyes. "The beneficial reason that hair grows on the rear end is severalfold. One, it prevents chafing of the buttock cheeks when you walk or run. As we all know, a chafed butt is a sorry situation. It also has a lovely evolutionary function. Ass hair holds in your natural scent. This is primal and something that attracts others."

"I'm gonna beg to differ on that," Lura Belle said with a sour expression. "A stinky bum is not attractive."

"I was right," Tory said, shaking her head.

About?" Gabe inquired with a chuckle.

The not-so-icy ice princess smirked, "That I would live to regret asking."

"Live and learn, motherfucker," Candy Vargo said with a laugh. "So, according to Timmy boy, unless y'all swallowed a portion of the ass containing the inferior gluteal artery, you're all good."

Lura Belle opened her mouth to say something else but changed her mind. She was smarter than she looked.

"How about this?" I suggested, wanting to move on to a new subject. "We'll watch the gals for unusual behavior and deal with it if we have to."

"Agreed," Candy Vargo said. "No use cryin' over spilt milk, bunghole arteries or stank hair up the poop shoot." The Keeper of Fate was always good for a disgusting visual that would stay in your frontal lobe for a while.

When the front door flew open, the gust of cold wind made me gasp with joy. Tears filled my eyes. There had been copious tears when Gabe and Prue reunited with Rafe and Abby. The siblings' love ran very deep, but that was nothing compared to the sobs of joy that left my mouth when I saw my baby.

"Special delivery," Jennifer announced with a wide smile as she handed me Alana Catherine. Missy, Amelia, June, Wally, Carl and Fred were right behind her.

Home was finally home. Alana Catherine's sleepy presence made it that way. I was pretty sure Gideon was crying more than me. So much for the Grim Reaper being the stoic bad guy...

"Now the gang is all here," I said with a grin so wide it hurt my cheeks. I held Alana Catherine as Gideon's strong arms wrapped around both of us. For the first time in a while, I was truly centered and calm.

"I want to hear everything," June announced as she beelined it for Charlie and gave him a kiss. "I'm just so happy everyone is home and safe."

"Oh yes, sweetikins," Carl squealed as he, Fred and Wally joined Dirk in a drag queen group hug. "We must hear the dish."

"Speaking of," Tim called out from the kitchen. "The

Turkey-Noodle-Dooda-Surprise hotdish is almost ready! Hope everyone is hungry. I've made four huge trays!"

"That does not sound good," Missy said before she grabbed Heather and soundly kissed her.

"We're going to the Piggly Wiggly in a sec for a more edible alternative," Heather told her.

Missy laughed. "I'm in."

Amelia glanced around in concern. "Where's Rafe?"

"Upstairs," Candy Vargo told her. "Go on up and kiss your man."

Amelia blushed. "Umm... okay, I think I will." She ran to the base of the stairs then turned back to her new roommate Candy. "Oh, the kids are great. I got everyone off to school this morning."

"Course you did," Candy said with a thumbs up. "You're the baddest of the badasses."

Amelia laughed and raced up the stairs.

"Love that gal like a daughter," Candy said, shaking her head. "Used to think I'd fucked over too many people to deserve anything good, but I got me a whole bunch of kids now. Who woulda thunk it?"

"I woulda thunk it," Gram said as she floated down the stairs with Mr. Jackson. "You might have a potty mouth and crappy manners, but you're as good as gold, Candy Vargo. It just tickles me pink to see you bein' a mamma to Amelia and all them darlin' foster kids. I'm right proud of you, girlie!"

It was the Keeper of Fate's turn to get teary-eyed.

June hustled over and put a large container on the coffee table in front of me. Life had just gone from perfect to out of this world.

"Is that what I think it is?" I asked, unable to contain my excitement.

13

June giggled. "If you think it's a tub of my homemade peanut butter cookies, then yes."

"I already ate a dozen this morning," Jennifer said with a laugh as she pulled a bottle of wine from her purse.

"Dude," I said, squinting at her. "Wine? Really?"

"It's five o'clock somewhere," she replied with a wink. "And I figured we might be having a celebration."

"Hell to the yes, Sugar Pants," Wally announced, snapping his fingers and producing a bottle opener. "I've been beside myself worried. A little vino would be welcome."

Fred and Carl, dressed to the nines in pink velvet mini dresses and heels, ran to the kitchen to get wine glasses for all.

Gideon chuckled and gave me a squeeze. "I suppose getting soused could make the turkey casserole tolerable."

"Not sure anything will make a combo of turkey, jelly, hot sauce and God only knows what else tolerable," I told him.

"I think I might have just thrown up in my mouth a little," Tory muttered with a pained laugh.

Heather stood up and grabbed her purse. "And on that note, I'm going to the Piggly Wiggly for donuts. Anybody in?"

"Ohhhh," Fred shrieked, coming back into the living room loaded down with wine glasses. "I'm in, doll face! The Piggly Wiggly is adorable. I picked up some Fruit Loops there last week."

"With what?" I asked with a wince.

Fred was perplexed. "My hands, girlfriend."

"Did you happen to pay for them or did you steal them?" I inquired. The queens weren't used to the social norms of the human world... like paying for things.

"Whoopsie doodle," Fred said with a giggle.

I shook my head and laughed. Alana Catherine cooed. She

had no clue what was going on, but joy was contagious... even if it was about pilfering Fruit Loops.

"Did you know that Fruit Loops are all the same flavor?" Jennifer asked as she poured the wine into the glasses.

"Blasphemy!" Wally cried out. "Is this true?"

"One hundred percent," Jennifer assured him. "Also, it's impossible to hum when you're holding your nose."

Of course, everyone in the room tested the theory. She was correct.

"I'm out," Heather said as she opened the front door.

"I'm coming, as well," Missy said.

"Us too!" Dirk exclaimed, hustling his three cohorts out of the door.

"Shall we?" June asked Charlie. "I could use some fresh air."

"We shall," Charlie said with a smile that made his adoration for his wife very clear.

"Well, heck," Jennifer said, topping off her wine glass. "If everyone's going, I ain't missin' out on a party!" She scurried out into the cold morning with a glass of wine in true Jennifer fashion.

The crowd had pared down, but it was still a happy home.

Looking down at Alana Catherine, my heart grew bigger. "I love you, baby girl."

Gideon leaned in and kissed her nose. Our gorgeous daughter reached up, grabbed a fistful of his hair and pulled. The Grim Reaper sighed in absolute contentment. Being a daddy was a good look on him.

"Not good. Not good. Not good," Dimple said in a shrill tone, jumping to her feet and walking in circles.

Jolly Sue got down on her hands and knees and began frantically searching for something on the floor. Lura Belle had gone ashen. She grabbed the arms of the love seat and began bouncing her knees spastically.

"What the fuck?" Candy Vargo muttered as she and Gabe rushed to the women.

Gideon immediately took Alana Catherine and covered her with his body. Gram and Mr. Jackson tried their best to calm the old gals, but nothing helped.

"What's happening?" I demanded, trying to get the Nephilim to talk to me.

"Don't know. Don't know," Dimple said, joining Jolly Sue on the floor.

"Might be the blood they got in their systems," Gabe said, doing his best to get them off the ground.

Tory, as depleted as she was, approached the panic-stricken old ladies and touched each one of them. Silver crystals formed a small funnel and rained gently down on the trio. Immediately, they grew serene. Gabe grabbed Tory's small frame before she collapsed. Cradling her in his arms, he gently placed her on the couch. His features were tight with concern.

Candy Vargo settled the Nephilim back on the loveseat and checked them over. Mr. Jackson and Gram hovered in the air over Tory.

I approached the gals and squatted down to their level. "Do you know what just happened?"

Lura Belle was still pale, but was more herself after Tory had touched her. "I don't. Just got a real bad feeling."

"Real bad," Jolly Sue added.

I glanced over at Candy Vargo.

She shook her head and shrugged. "Don't know." She pulled a handful of toothpicks out and shoved them into her mouth. "Most likely it's a reaction to the blood."

The front door opened, and Heather walked inside. "I'm back."

"That was fast," I said.

She laughed. "Wasn't enough room in the car," she replied, looking around. "What's happening here?"

My phone vibrated in my pocket. I ignored it. I was glad for the extra backup on whatever was going on with the Nephilim. I welcomed my sister's intelligence and intuition. Maybe she could figure out what the hell was happening. "Not exactly sure," I informed her. "They just started acting strange a few seconds ago. Tory tried to help, but her energy is too far drained at this point."

Heather assessed the situation and moved to a very weak and pale Tory. "Get up," she told Gabe. "I want to check her over."

Gabe stood and joined me by the Nephilim. His body was tense and leaving Tory didn't make him happy. However, Heather had powers that could help her. Gabe wouldn't stand in our sister's way.

Tim popped his head into the living room. I was surprised he hadn't heard the ruckus. "Where did everyone go? Food's almost ready."

"Piggly Wiggly," I said, then quickly added. "I think they went to get some dessert." Hurting Tim's feelings wasn't on the table.

My pocket kept buzzing. I briefly wondered if they got to the Piggly Wiggly and had no money. The thought was absurd. While the queens might have sticky fingers, the rest of my crew were law-abiding citizens.

"You got a vibratin' dildo in your pants or are you just happy to see me?" Candy inquired with a chuckle.

"Nope," I said with a grin as I pulled out my phone and glanced at it.

I read the text once. Confused, I read it again. Then I read it once more.

My body felt hot. The phone felt like a venomous snake in my hand. My brain raced, and my stomach tightened to the point of pain. Breathing was difficult, and I pulled from all the power I possessed to stay calm.

"Gideon," I said in an outwardly relaxed tone while my insides screamed in terror. "Alana Catherine needs her diaper changed. Can you take her up and change it, please?"

"Happy to," he said, not noticing my inner freakout.

That was good. If he didn't notice, there was no way anyone else did.

Glancing down at the phone again, I prayed hard that I'd misconstrued what I'd seen. I hadn't. It was a text message from Heather at the Piggly Wiggly asking if I wanted blueberry donuts as well as glazed. Heather was at the store... but she was also on the couch with Tory, and no one else was in reaching distance except for two ghosts who wouldn't be much help if shit hit the fan.

My fingers began to spark, and my hair blew wildly around my head.

It wasn't Heather sitting on my couch, not unless she could magically be in two places at once. The sick feeling in the pit of my stomach grew until I thought it would swallow me up.

"You okay?" Doppelganger-Heather asked.

I stared at her, trying to keep the rage and fear out of my eyes. "What's the safe word?"

She looked confused.

I didn't back down. My upper lip curled into a snarl. "Tell me the safe word. Now."

Candy Vargo growled deep in her throat. Gabe hissed as his wings burst from his back, and his eyes went blindingly gold. Heather laughed and wrapped her arms around Tory. Her grip was vise-like as Tory tried to move away.

"Tell me the safe word," I ground out.

In less time than it took to inhale, Heather was gone, and Micky Muggles was in her place. He was naked, and he held a razor-sharp sword to Tory's neck. "Don't make a move, or your little buddy is dust," he threatened.

"What do you want?" I snapped.

The blade was too close to Tory's neck to attack, and she was too weak to fight him off. The sound of fury and agony that came from Gabe chilled me to the bone.

"Immortality," Micky Muggles said. "Isn't that what everyone wants?"

"You ain't got nowhere to store the magic," Candy Vargo hissed. "We removed your tail. You're done, fucker." Sparks popped off of her. "It's only a matter of time." She looked like a deadly crate of fireworks about to explode in every direction and light this place up.

"And that's where you're wrong, bitch," Micky Muggles shot back with an oily laugh. He grabbed his dick with his free hand and stroked it. "The tail is in the front."

Lura Belle stepped forward with Dimple and Jolly Sue at her side. "You take your hands off Tory, you paunchy, ruttish wagtail," she shouted.

"Or what?" he demanded with a raised brow.

"Or you'll regret it with every fiber of your slimy being," I ground out, looking for an opening to blast him without harming Tory.

Gram and Mr. Jackson had attached themselves to Tory to give her comfort. Micky Muggles pressed the sword into

Tory's neck. The blade cut into her flesh, and it appeared sharp enough that it wouldn't take much if he wanted to decapitate her.

The shitshow unfolding in front of me was the worst I'd ever experienced. With all the power and magic I had, I was helpless. *How did a psychotic redneck Nephilim with a mullet keep besting us?*

"Here's the deal," Micky said with a wink and a wank. "You figure out how to get Parveit, Lord the Red, true Immortality. I'm gettin' right sick of drinkin' blood all the time."

"And?" I pressed.

"And I won't drain this powerful little Immortal dry," he bargained with a chuckle. The scum leaned over and licked some of the blood gushing from Tory's neck. "Yum. Tasty." He smacked his lips together grossly. "You got one week."

He was a stupid egomaniac. My brain worked overtime to use the knowledge to my advantage. "A week should be enough time," I told him, sounding as casual as I could considering the circumstances. "Where can we find you when we have the spell?"

I was beyond sure that a spell for Immortality didn't exist. However, I was banking on his lack of brain cells and his greed.

"Read the book," he shouted. "It's in the fucking book."

In a blast of dull brown dust, the vile self-proclaimed dragon disappeared with Tory.

Gabe's anguished bellow of fury brought everyone from upstairs racing to the living room. Candy Vargo grabbed Tim, removed him from the kitchen and detonated it. We were lucky the entire house didn't collapse.

"What's going on?" Gideon demanded, holding a crying Alana Catherine in his arms.

"Micky Muggles took Tory," Gabe roared.

"How?" Zander demanded. "He shouldn't have had that much power left."

The Keeper of Fate, still glowing dangerously, answered the question. "The dragon's tail wasn't his ass. It's his dick."

The information caused a moment of appalled silence. My fury and terror for Tory made me itch. I wanted to peel my skin off my body. That would be a bad move. I was going to save that torture for Micky Muggles.

"You've read the book," I said to Candy. "Where would Parveit, Lord of the Red hang out for a week?"

Candy's smile was dastardly. To me, it was gorgeous. "Kentucky. Lexington, Kentucky."

"Wait. Where are Gram and Mr. Jackson?" Prue asked.

The need to throw up was real. "Gram?" I called out. "Mr. Jackson? I need you to show yourselves. Now. Please."

Nothing.

Gabe punched a hole in the plaster then walked to the center of the gathered group. "I'm leaving. I want the Nephilim and Candy Vargo with me. The Nephilim can feel the bastard's presence. I'm sure that's why they freaked out." Gabe's wings vibrated with power. His golden eyes narrowed to slits. "I will find him, and I will end him."

The front door opened and the crew from the Piggly Wiggly entered. Their gazes immediately fell upon the golden-glowing Archangel. He was lit up like a Christmas tree, and he had the floor.

"What did we miss?" Heather asked, feeling the dark mood.

"Micky Muggles took Tory and possibly Gram and Mr. Jackson," I filled them in.

"Where?" Charlie demanded.

"Lexington, Kentucky," Candy answered.

I looked into the Immortal Enforcer's eyes. "Tell me the safe word."

"Toothpick," Charlie replied without hesitation.

I took Alana Catherine from Gideon's arms and handed her to Charlie. "Take her back to Candy's. Drop a ward around the house and protect her with your life."

"As you wish," Charlie said, disappearing in a haze of silver mist.

"The rest of you stay here. If Gram or Mr. Jackson show up, call me," I ordered.

"We're going to Kentucky?" Gideon asked.

"Yep," I said, taking his hand in mine then reaching for Gabe's. "It's time to slay the dragon for good."

This time, there would be no mercy.

CHAPTER TWO

WE FORMED THE CIRCLE QUICKLY. MY MIND WAS JUMBLED WITH alarm. The entire scene felt chaotic and wrong. Even Gideon was hesitant. Gabe seemed ready to combust. His entire body trembled with rage. We were a hot mess ready to turn into a shitshow on a dime.

"Hang the fuck on for a sec," Candy Vargo grunted as we prepared to transport. Picking her ear with a toothpick that had formerly been in her mouth, she paced the living room like a caged tiger. "Now, I'm all for heading to Kentucky and ripping Micky Muggle's innards out and shoving them down his throat, but we ain't got no plan. Don't know where we're goin'. Don't know what we're doin'. Don't know shit."

She'd made an excellent observation, and my sigh of relief was audible. I was getting used to winging it, but that luck was bound to run out eventually. It was tempting to remove the toothpick from her hand, but getting electrocuted was something I didn't have time for. Instead, I addressed her concern. "Do you have a plan?"

The Keeper of Fate rolled her eyes. "Nope. But here's how I

see it. Life's become a fuckin' creamy messy shit symphony, and I don't wanna be the fecal-covered conductor. You feel me?"

I closed my eyes and swallowed back my bile. No one could accuse Candy Vargo of not being graphically repulsive. If Gram were here, she'd give Candy a piece of her mind for such a colorful and disgusting analogy.

Gram wasn't here. I had a very bad feeling that she and the sweet, dead Mr. Jackson were with Tory and Micky Muggles.

"All shit comparisons aside, Candy has a point," Heather admitted, pressing the bridge of her nose. "Of course, her delivery had the grace of a cow on stilts."

"Thank you," Candy said.

It was Heather's turn to roll her eyes. "Wasn't a compliment."

"Whatever," Candy shot back, flipping Heather off.

"Going in blind without a semblance of a strategy is a disaster in the making," Gideon stated flatly.

"This is absurd," Gabe ground out with his eyes glowing a furious gold. "We're wasting time. We will leave NOW."

Gideon eyed my brother then put his hand on his shoulder to calm him. Gabe didn't have a shred of composure at the moment. He knocked the Grim Reaper's hand away, walked to the fireplace and glared daggers at everyone in the room.

Gideon's voice was firm. "We're on your side, Archangel Gabriel. If you fight your own army, you will lose."

My brother's body was tense, and his expression was terrifying, but he wasn't a stupid man. He nodded curtly at Gideon before he dropped his gaze.

I blew out a breath, hoping Gabe's love for Tory would keep his temper in check. The Archangel flying off the rails would turn the shitshow into a shitstorm, and that was the last thing we needed right now. I would keep a close eye on my brother. Tory wasn't the only one in jeopardy. Gram's un-life was at stake, along with poor Mr. Jackson's.

"Candy Vargo," Gideon said, all business. "In the book, where in Lexington, Kentucky did it say the piece of shit dragon would go?"

Thank God someone was making sense. Gideon to the rescue. The Grim Reaper was a brilliant badass with an excellent butt.

And he was mine.

Candy shrugged. "Book wasn't too specific," she admitted.

Tim raised his hand. "We mustn't forget that Agnes' books were fiction."

"With a whole lot of unbelievable truth on the pages," I reminded him, then turned my attention to the Keeper of Fate who now was digging in both of her ears with toothpicks. At the rate she was going she'd be deaf or bleeding from her eardrums in five minutes. She was Immortal. She'd heal, but it would be gross. I wasn't up for gross right now. Gabe might be hanging on by a thread, but I wasn't far behind. If Gram got destroyed in the crossfire of Micky Muggles' insanity, I would lose my debatably sane mind. "Candy. Think. Is there a chapter that talks about Lexington, Kentucky?"

It would save one hell of a lot of time if we knew where we were going. I'd never been to Kentucky, but I was pretty sure Lexington was one of the bigger cities in the state.

"Nah," she said. "It was kind of a one-off in the epilogue. Says the dragon was off to Kentucky to live in his castle."

The trio of sisters, Dimple, Jolly Sue and Lura Belle snorted with disgust.

"Makes sense. I'll bet the mangled, clay-brained, logger-headed clotpole insisted on that part," Dimple snapped.

"Agreed," Lura Belle growled, her cat-butt lips on full display. "The impertinent, beslubbering hedge pig has delusions of grandeur."

"Ohhhhhh yessssss," Jolly Sue added with a shudder. "The reeky nut-hook's obsessions are many."

My skin tingled. In my gut, I was positive the Nephilim had just said something important in between the off-color, centuries-old insults. The three old gals were a mess from the transport home, but somehow, they were still strangely put together. With their new lease on life, after their evil curses were removed, they were the opposite of who they'd been only yesterday. All three were very well preserved and expertly coiffed seventy-somethings—who were actually much older. They dressed conservatively and expensively in designer duds. Their newly found improved personalities didn't erase that they were still pains in the ass, but I'd go to bat for them any day of the week.

"Darlings!" Dirk chimed in, clapping his well-manicured hands with delight. "Do tell. It sounds quite juicy."

"I agree with Dirk," I said quickly. "Can you expand on what you just shared?"

Lura Belle stepped forward. She was the unofficial leader of the trio. "Of course," she replied. "Before the fly-bitten mold warp fancied himself a dragon, he used to believe he was the king."

"Of England," Dimple chimed in. "Told any fool who would listen that he was the reincarnation of King Henry."

"The eighth?" Tim asked, paling.

I sucked in a breath and waited for the answer. King Henry the Eighth liked to decapitate his wives. Micky Muggles wasn't married to Tory, but he was unhinged enough to do something heinous to her.

"Yes. King Henry the Eighth," Jolly Sue confirmed with hiss of disgust. "That pribbling lewdster is batshit crazy."

"Oh yes! Oh yes!" Dimple said. "I concur. If there's a castle in Lexington, Kentucky, that's where the bootless beetle-headed puckling is hiding."

Lura Belle bared her teeth. The very same teeth that had been instrumental in biting off Micky Muggles' ass only hours ago. "I say we find the castle and castrate the mewling maggot-pie. Because you beautiful people have given me and my sisters your friendship and trust, we will be honored to remove the offending pecker with our teeth."

"We will?" Jolly Sue gasped out, turning a bit green.

"Umm... I'm not so sure about that," Dimple said with a wince. The poor old woman looked like she was about to empty the contents of her stomach again.

Without a second thought, Lura Belle whipped around in her sensible, low-heeled leather pumps and decked both of her sisters with a right hook and a left jab that would have been impressive on a pay-per-view boxing match. I couldn't believe the old gals hadn't been knocked down for the count. The gift of magic that my Angel siblings had given them recently was still coursing strongly through them. Otherwise, they would have been unconscious.

That was a good thing. They weren't technically Immortal, but with the extra power, they'd be better able to defend themselves in a fight.

And there was going to be a fight. I felt it in my bones.

No one in the living room batted an eye at the geriatric violence. We were getting used to the gals' smackdowns.

"Okay," I said, crossing the room and pulling Jolly Sue and Dimple back to their feet. "I'm about to speak aloud a sentence I never in my wildest dreams thought I would utter." I sighed

27

and shook my head. "As much as I appreciate you being willing to bite Micky Muggles'... umm... pecker off, I think castration by teeth should be the very last resort."

Candy Vargo offered me a toothpick. I politely declined. Since I couldn't be sure it wasn't the one she'd been digging for ear wax with, I wasn't taking any chances.

"Normally," Candy stated, patting each of the Nephilim on the head with what I guessed was respect, "I really enjoy some good bloody dismemberment, but I have to admit that even though the thought of you fuckers gnawing off that son of a bitch's salami is amusing, not sure I could watch that shit without losing my cookies. I fuckin' hate puking. So, I'm agreeing with Daisy on this one. No biting off the rod. I vote for loppin' it off with a sword then makin' him eat it."

No one had anything to add to that. Candy was a weapon of mass indigestion.

"Alrighty then. I've got some good-ish news," Jennifer chimed in, pulling the ever-present bottle of wine from her bag. "I used to live in Lexington, Kentucky. Back in the day I went to college at UK and drank my way into a BS degree in Communications. Used to chug for my sorority. I could drink those frat boys under the table." She poured herself a glass of wine then took a swig from the bottle. "Pretty sure I still could."

"Werk, girlfriend." Fred, in full fabulous drag, gave her two snaps up and finished with a gimme gesture.

My human friend gave the Immortal drag queen a thumbs up as she handed him the bottle.

College binge-drinking aside, I wasn't sure her story was pertinent to our current situation. "How is this good-ish news?"

She gave me a look that I'm sure would've been a raised

brow if Jennifer had been capable of the move. "Sorry! I own an Airbnb there." She scratched her head. "Probably should've led with that. Got custody of that during my second divorce. It's a nice passive income."

"You've never told me that story," I said. I'd known Jennifer for a decade, and I was amazed that there were still new things to learn about my splendid friend.

"I have a controversial and diverse past. It would take a lifetime of girls' nights and a lot of wine to get through it." She shrugged. "We should actually use the place in Kentucky sometime for a gals' getaway. It's dang nice. Tim, you'd love it. It has a nice big kitchen."

"Ohhhh, sounds lovely!" Tim said, clasping his hands together. "I'd quite enjoy going to the Kentucky Derby at some point."

"Been there. Done that," Jennifer shared. "Although, I have to admit, mint juleps taste like assy medicine. I'm not a bourbon girl—more of a wine drinker." With that obvious admission, she took the bottle back from Fred and sucked back a healthy gulp.

"Is *any* of this conversation necessary?" Gabe demanded, looking like he was going to do property damage. "While you're planning your next vacation, Muggles is doing whatever he wants to—" His voice caught as he stopped just short of voicing his worst fears.

I gave my brother a sympathetic nod. He wasn't wrong, though. We needed to get back to the matter at hand.

"Gabe," Candy Vargo said in a monotone, idly twirling a toothpick in her fingers. It was pretty scary. "At the risk of you attacking me, which would lead me to attacking you back, I'm gonna ask you to shut your fuckin' cake hole. I understand your fury. I respect it. But you know as well as I do that words have meaning, and rarely do conversations happen randomly. I'd suggest you listen to the fuckin' words and pull your head out of your ass crack. You ain't gonna do Tory no good if you're a shlong."

My brother inhaled deeply before exhaling audibly.

I put my hand on his shoulder and said to Candy, "Fine point."

My brother finished with a grudging, "Well, made."

I couldn't blame my brother for his anger or fear. I had plenty of both, but the Keeper of Fate was the Keeper for a reason. If she thought there was something important being said, then we would damn well listen.

"That's right, motherfuckers," Candy said with a grunt and a grin. "Just hang on. We're gonna get where we need to be shortly." The Keeper of Fate nodded to me. "Keep talkin', Daisy."

"Do you know of a castle in Lexington?" I asked Jennifer, hoping it wasn't a figment of Agnes' fertile imagination. Our dearly departed author buddy had one heck of a wild mild.

Jennifer nodded as she dug into the Piggly Wiggly doughnuts. "There was one back when I was in college all those years ago. Pretty sure it's still there. It was out Versailles Road—pronounced phonetically, by the way—ver-sales."

Gideon took a doughnut from the box and led Jennifer to the couch. "A real castle?"

She chuckled. "A real castle. Some guy built it for his wife after they went to Europe or something like that. They got a divorce before it was finished. Typical—just like sex with most of my exes. I think it's gone through a couple of owners and from what I heard, it turned into some kind of wedding venue and hotel thingie. That is, if it's still there."

Tim pulled out his laptop and typed like a madman. "Here

it is! Kentucky Castle. It exists. Construction had started in 1969 by real estate developer Rex Martin and his wife. It was inspired by a trip to Germany and buildings they'd seen in Europe. Divorced in 1975 and left the castle—which was supposed to have seven bedrooms and fifteen bathrooms—unfinished."

"They must have had poop shoot issues," Candy Vargo muttered. "Ain't nobody needs fifteen fuckin' bathrooms unless you have a very active bunghole and tend to clog your crappers with crap."

"I'm not touching that comment, Candy Vargo," Tim chided her as he continued to read the information. "Over the years it became a tourist destination and appears to be somewhat of a joke for the locals. Martin died before it sold, but it eventually was bought and was rumored to become some kind of medieval restaurant or museum. In 2004, it caught fire, and the owner rebuilt it. It was completed in 2008. Twelve luxury suites were added along with a game room, music room, swimming pool, basketball court and tennis courts. It was used for events. It was sold again in 2017 and is still used for events."

"Well, shoot," Heather said. "If that's where he is, humans will be in danger."

"If we were there, he'd be dead," Gabe snapped. "Tory would be alive, and no humans would be harmed. BUT... we're NOT there."

"I told you to relax your fuckin' crack, Archangel," Candy Vargo warned. "We have a week. The stupid fuck wants immortality real bad. He's not gonna eliminate his bargainin' chip, and with his ass gone, he's going to spend most of that time healing up."

"On Tory's blood!" Gabe countered.

My brother had a point. The longer it took us to take Micky Muggles down, the stronger he was going to get on his Purgatory diet, and that assless bastard was already pretty fucking powerful. He'd proved that when he walked into a room full of Immortals and snatched one of us without even trying.

The Keeper of Fate pulled a clean toothpick from the box. "If we go in guns blazin' we're gonna lose." She shoved the slender pick between her teeth as she narrowed her gaze at Gabe. "I'm not thinkin' you wanna lose. I know I sure as hell don't. Gram, Tory, and that weird, nice dead guy need us to stay fuckin' focused."

Gabe let out a frustrated growl as he punched the wall and put his fist through the plaster. At the rate my house was being demolished, Gideon and I were going to need to move. Although, Gabe was on to something. In the last few months, I'd realized property damage was cathartic.

"We'll drive," Gideon said. "It's less conspicuous, and we can strategize on the way. Transporting with a group would mean a tremendous amount of mind-wiping, and it would alert every supernatural in the area when we arrived. Including Muggles. That's a bad idea and one we don't have time for."

"I agree." I ran my hands through my hair, doing my best to focus like Candy had insisted. My mind raced with worry for Gram, Tory and Mr. Jackson. I'd seen ghosts get destroyed and turned to dust. Although, I hoped Micky Muggles wasn't too concerned with two dead people. They couldn't help him with his psychotic goal. However, he could use them as bargaining chips. My other worry was my baby. It wasn't an over exaggeration to say I'd barely seen her since I'd given birth. It wasn't working for me. But my life had been spiraling out of control lately. While I hadn't signed up to be an Immortal badass, I would play the hand I'd been dealt.

Right now, it sucked. Hard.

Tim's fingers flew across his keyboard. "The drive is nine hours give or take a few minutes. Do we have a big enough vehicle for everyone going?"

Gabe punched the wall again. He was ignored.

"I have a minivan," Candy volunteered. "I can drive."

"Hard no from me," I said, shaking my head. I'd been a passenger in Candy's car. She drove like a blind person and at least fifty miles over the speed limit. "We can take your minivan, but you are *not* driving."

"Excellent thinking," Tim agreed, trying to hide his smile. He failed. "Candy Vargo is a menace on the road."

"And all of the rest of the time as well," Heather added with a grin.

"Fuck all you fuckers," Candy said with a hint of a smirk pulling at her lips.

Up until now some of our group had been silent. June, Amelia, Missy, my other siblings and two of the Queens had just watched and listened. Ameila, Rafe, Abby and Prue sat on the ground with my furbabies, Donna and Karen. Donna wasn't a dog even though she looked like one. She was a Hell Hound. Her ears were perked up as she listened to the conversation. Karen was a dopey lab. I adored both of my beautiful furry girls.

June walked over to the table, picked up the Tupperware container of peanut butter cookies and handed them to me. "You're gonna need these, sweetie," she said with a smile. "And I think you all should stay at Jennifer's Airbnb."

"Darn tootin'," Jennifer agreed. "You want me to come?"

I mulled that over in my head. Jennifer was human. Shockingly, when she'd discovered none of us were even remotely human, she'd believed it instantly and took no issue. She was simply disappointed that we didn't sparkle like the vampires in the *Twilight* series.

"How well do you know Lexington?" Gideon asked before I could arrive at a decision.

"Damn good," Jennifer told him. "And after the gals bite off that bastard's wiener and you guys save Tory, Gram and Mr. Jackson, I can take y'all by my old sorority house and we can chug a few beers for old time's sake."

"Or not," I said with a wince. "Not sure taking Jen is safe."

Dirk, Fred, Wally and Carl—also known as the Four Horsemen of the Apocalypse—stepped forward in all their beaded and bejeweled glory.

"Sweetikins," Carl said in a serious tone. "If a gift is offered, you must take it."

Wally chimed in. "Sugar Pants, Carl not only looks divine in his feathered frock, he's correct. As the Keeper of Fate said, one must listen. Things like gifts rarely occur without reason."

"Girlfriend," Fred said, sashaying over and taking my hand. "Don't worry your gorgeous little head about the brave and oft-married Jennifer. We shall ride our horses to Lexington, Kentucky and protect her."

My eyes widened. "Umm... not sure that's a great plan. Kind of conspicuous. I mean, four drag queens on horses is pretty noticeable."

"Dollface has a point," Dirk said, tossing the long locks of his wig over his broad shoulders. "Maybe we should drive."

"Fabulous!" Carl squealed.

"Wait," I said, holding up a hand. "Do any of you know how to drive? Do any of you have a driver's license?"

"What's that?" Wally inquired, confused.

I groaned. The guys didn't carry money. They pilfered items when they went shopping. Why I thought they might have driver's licenses was beyond me.

Tim closed his laptop with a snap. "I have an idea," he announced.

"Speak, mail boy," Candy Vargo commanded.

Tim tucked his computer into his mailbag and pulled a pad of paper and pen from one of his many pockets. He jotted as he spoke. "Heather, Prue, Abby and Rafe shall stay here and protect Missy, Amelia and June."

"Likin' it so far," Candy said.

I rolled my eyes. So far, this wasn't much of a plan.

Tim continued. "The minivan seats eight comfortably with room for small suitcases in the back. I'd suggest that Gideon, Daisy, Candy, Gabe, Lura Belle, Jolly Sue, Dimple and Jennifer ride in the van. I shall follow behind in my mail truck with Dirk, Fred, Wally and Carl."

"Will our horses fit in the mail truck?" Dirk inquired.

"Umm… no," Tim replied much to the disappointment of the Four Horsemen. "Even though Lexington, Kentucky is the horse capital of the world, I think that if you ride your over-sized stallions through the streets of town, we might end up incarcerated."

"Interesting," Carl said. "Humans are such an odd and judgmental crew."

I agreed with Carl's statement about humans, but agreed more with Tim's opinion that the horses should be left behind. "A bigger group will make it more difficult to stay under the radar. Micky Muggles knows all of us. If he feels backed into a corner, there's no telling what the asshole will do."

"One," Tim said, holding up a finger. "He has no ass at the moment. The Nephilim removed it with their teeth."

"Sure did," Lura Belle crowed, pumping her bony fists above her head.

Dimple and Jolly Sue just nodded and gagged.

"Two," Tim continued. "There is no reason at all that we have to *look like* ourselves."

Candy Vargo laughed. "Point for the mail fucker. Not sayin' he fornicates with the mail. I meant it in a nice way."

I gritted my teeth together. "Candy, you should probably stop talking."

"Roger that," she replied.

I turned to Tim, who wasn't the least bothered by his buddy Candy's foul mouth. "Can you be more specific?" I asked. The Immortals were cryptic, but Tim usually came through with an answer I could understand.

Tim smiled and nodded. "Daisy, if you recall, Candy Vargo altered her appearance when we were dealing with the police whilst breaking into Agnes' house. She went from sloppy and somewhat normal looking—albeit beautiful—to sloppy and somewhat rotund. Of course, still lovely."

"Rotund is fuckin' polite. I was over five hundred pounds," Candy said with a chuckle. "But that bein' said... and thank you, Tim, for recognizing my hotness at any size, I can make us all rotund and unrecognizable. No worries there."

I did recall what Tim was talking about. Rotund was putting it mildly. While disguises would be smart, I wasn't as sure if we should all be over five hundred pounds.

"How long will the disguises hold?" Gideon asked.

I gave him a quick glance. Did he seriously think this was a good idea?

"Bout twelve hours," Candy confirmed.

"And is rotund the only disguise you're capable of?" Gideon pressed as I heaved a sigh of relief.

"Nope, fucker," Candy assured the Grim Reaper. "I can do any size, any sex, any height, any build. I'd only gone with that size so that the fuckers we were distracting would have trouble moving me out of there. I'd even added another thousand pounds of magical weight for good measure."

"OH MY GOD!" Carl squealed as if having an epiphany... possibly a seizure. "Does this mean I can have a real and luscious bosom for twelve hours?"

The other three Horsemen bounced up and down in their heels in rabid excitement.

"Yep," Candy confirmed.

The screaming was loud. It took a light electrocution from me to get the guys to calm down. I was a bit worried they'd be more invested in their breasts than protecting Jennifer but decided to cross that bouncy bridge when we got to it.

Heather glanced over at the still-seething Gabe, then checked her watch. "I say everyone takes an hour to pack and get ready. I'm going to grab some burner phones from my place and hand them out. I'd suggest packing lightly. Magic can be used sparingly if you need extra items."

"Oh yes!" Tim said, heading to the front door. "I'll also have room in the truck for any luggage that won't fit in the minivan."

Gideon cleared his throat and garnered everyone's attention. "The hour starts now. Candy Vargo, I'd suggest you repair the kitchen you blew up."

"Suggest or order?" Candy shot back with a grin.

Gideon simply raised a brow.

"On it," the Keeper of Fate said with a laugh.

I looked around the room. I loved every person in it. As crazy as life had become, I realized I would change very little of it. What-ifs were a waste of time we didn't have. It was time to bring Tory, Gram and Mr. Jackson home. It was far past time to end Micky Muggles' reign of terror. "Everyone, move it. We have fifty-nine minutes."

And on that note, we dispersed and got ready for the upcoming battle. My fingers were crossed that it would be a successful, small and short skirmish.

I wasn't counting on it.

CHAPTER THREE

METHODICALLY PACKING KEPT ME MOMENTARILY SANE. FEELING somewhat desperate and lost didn't help, but I just kept moving forward. Doing something that didn't hinge on the world ending was rare for me lately. I shoved sweats, one nice outfit with boots, underwear and an extra pair of tennis shoes into a duffle then added toiletries. The weight of the mission ahead weighed heavy on my shoulders. Picking up a cute stuffed teddy bear belonging to my daughter, I hugged it to my chest and finally let the enormity of everything hit me hard.

The tears came unbidden. Hiding them was impossible. My anguish, fear and uncertainty came flooding out. I didn't even see the Grim Reaper move. His arms were around me in an instant and he held me tight.

"It will be okay, Daisy," Gideon whispered into my hair.

His voice was calm. His embrace was needed. His tone was comforting, but words didn't cut it right now.

"Will it?" My voice was muffled as I cried into his chest and soaked his shirt. "And even if it is, what's next? It hasn't stopped. Not even for a moment."

I'd turned forty and my world had changed irrevocably. On the last day of my thirty-ninth year, I'd been a widowed paralegal. Now, I was that and much more. The first day of my fortieth year, I began to see dead people. Then I realized I could glue them together and help them move on into the afterlife. I entered their minds to aid them, which permanently altered my DNA, making me Immortal. That had taken some getting used to. It still did. Then, much to my horror, I added Angel of Mercy to my resume. I took shit on the daily from Candy Vargo and a few others for not having read the Bible. It was on my to-do list... along with about a million other things. But the point of all of it was that the deadly missions hadn't slowed down.

Yes, I'd fallen in love with Gideon. For real. I had my miracle baby. When Gram died, she'd come back as a ghost and stayed with me. That was a gift that I was beyond grateful for. I'd been blessed to get to know my birth father and my deceased mother came back to me for a short time—too short, but it was another gift I would cherish always. However, I was going to break soon.

I wasn't sure how much more I could take. Of course, I was going to take on getting Tory, Gram and Mr. Jackson back full throttle, but after that... I just didn't know. Less than a year ago, I was a mortal, middle-aged woman with bills and a mundane job. A tiny part of me longed for that simplicity again, but that was gone.

Gideon sighed and rested his chin on my head. "It won't always be like this. I've gone centuries with nothing to do."

"That would be seriously nice," I choked out, wiping my eyes with his already wet shirt. "We have a child who doesn't know us."

"Alana Catherine knows us," he promised. "She recognizes us at a bone-deep level."

I was about to argue, but I wanted to believe him, so I just let it go.

What I wanted to do was run. Not away from it all, but just a few miles to knock the chaos out of my mind. Running for fun and exercise had always been my go-to when I was stressed. Lately, I'd been running toward danger for my and everyone else's well-being. The thought of going for a pleasure jog was silly, but I needed some normal.

"Tell me what you want," Gideon said, lifting my chin and staring straight into my eyes.

His beauty still startled me. However, his insides were more beautiful than his outer exterior. My other half was the ridiculous kind of handsome—tall and built with full kissable lips, gray-blue eyes and sexy messy blond hair. Although, he was millions of years old, the man looked to be about forty-five. Wrapping my head around his true age was something I'd leave for another time. His life as the Grim Reaper had not been an easy or joyful one. However, he'd also made good use of his downtime—so to speak. He'd attended college and grad school multiple times, and over the years, he'd worked as a doctor, social worker, human rights activist, professor of philosophy, firefighter, sculptor, chef and dog trainer. Those occupations were the ones I knew of. It also delighted me that his favorite of all his jobs had been as a dog trainer.

The man was a keeper. I just wanted to live long enough to be able to keep him. Yes, I was Immortal, but that didn't mean I couldn't die. I was just harder to kill. Decapitation killed even the strongest of the Immortals.

"Tell me, baby," Gideon whispered, looking concerned. "What can I do to make you feel better?"

There was no time for a run. I knew seeing Alana Catherine before we left was out of the question too. Right now, in this moment, I wasn't sure what he could do. However, I could do something. I would make plans for the future. Having something to look forward to meant that I believed we would all come out of the next twenty-four to forty-eight hours in one piece. At least, that was the story I was going with.

"A vacation," I told him.

Gideon tilted his head His expression was one of confusion. "Now?"

"Nope. The minute this is over... after we've won. I want you, Alana Catherine and me to get the hell out of dodge. I want to go somewhere sunny where there's a beach and a crystal-clear ocean. I want to drink pina coladas and not wear shoes for a week... or maybe two. I don't want to think about the world ending or who wants me dead. I want to have sex every single time our baby takes a nap and multiple times each night. I want pancakes for dinner and dessert for breakfast."

Gideon's grin was wide and his laugh made me lose my breath. His laugh and happiness were like a drug to me that I needed to survive.

"I do believe I can make that happen," he said, pressing his lips to mine and making me forget my name for a hot sec. "I have a place on the French Riviera that will fit the bill. If that doesn't appeal, I have another in Turks and Caicos or another in Thailand."

I squinted at him. "How many *places* do you have?" It was easy to forget he was older than dirt and richer than Midas.

"Lots," he said with a chuckle as he grabbed both his and my duffle bags. "Enough that we could go a year or so and spend a week at each without repeating a stay."

"Dude," I said with a whistle. "You should probably have me sign a prenup before we get hitched."

Gideon stopped dead in his tracks. He slowly turned back to me. His eyes lit up red with desire and his expression made my panties damp. "Did you just ask me to marry you, Daisy?"

My mouth dropped open into a perfect O... and then I laughed. It sounded a little unhinged even to my own ears. I was a modern woman. Gender roles were silly. But... "Umm... I think I might have." I began to fidget as his gaze bored into mine. It was impossible to tell what he was thinking. Had I said something stupid? I mean, we already had a baby and a home together. Yes, he was the Grim Reaper and I was the Angel of Mercy, but did that matter? Maybe Demons didn't do human rituals. Maybe I was an idiot of epic proportions.

I stuttered as I backtracked. "Umm... we don't... you know... ahh... have to do that. No worries. None at all. I was just joshing you. Cause... umm... That was crazy. I'm crazy. So... umm... if we could just erase that and, you know..."

The smile on his lips started slowly. It became full as he listened to my mini freak out. By the time I was finished, he was down on one knee.

I clapped my hand over my mouth to keep from squealing as my stomach turned somersaults. I felt like I was having an out-of-body experience. The timing was odd since we were about to go to what basically amounted to war, but nothing in my life was normal anymore. I was learning to take happiness where I could get it.

This was all kinds of happy.

"There's nothing more in this world I'd like to do than marry you, Daisy Leigh Amara Jones," he said, snapping his fingers and producing an engagement ring so exquisite I gasped. It wasn't huge. It was perfect for me. The diamond was pink surrounded by a cluster of small white diamonds. The band was platinum with delicate scrolls. "There will be no prenup," he continued as he slid the ring onto my shaking finger. It fit. No surprise there. "Because we will be together until the end of time. Everything material I have means nothing. Only you and Alana Catherine make me feel alive. So... yes. I will marry you."

I couldn't help myself. I checked the time on my phone. We had thirty-three more minutes. So I did what any newly engaged forty-year-old woman who was in love with her man would do.

I jumped him.

His bellow of laughter as I removed his clothes was music to my ears. I ripped off my own even quicker. To say he was happy to see me would have been an understatement.

"Bed. Now," Gideon said gruffly as he picked me up and tossed me onto the mattress. "I have an issue that only you can solve."

I eyed his impressive package and grinned. "I know just the thing to solve that issue. Come over here and let me work on that."

"With pleasure."

The sex was fast, furious and mind-blowing. It was also life-affirming and glorious. Sex was great. Sex combined with love was simply beyond. Two freaking orgasms in twenty-seven minutes. Hell to the yes. Gideon's body becoming one with mine was what we both needed. His love for me and mine for him was all that mattered.

"Holy hell," I wheezed out as we lay side by side after what felt like the best lovemaking of my life. Quickies were vastly underrated. Being the parents of a baby, the quickie was going to be our new hobby, and I was all for it.

He chuckled. "My thoughts exactly. Up," he said, pulling me to my feet with the expression of a very satisfied man. "We have three minutes to get downstairs."

"Not sure I can walk," I muttered with a laugh as I grabbed my clothes. "You're really good at that."

He raised a brow. "Only with my fiancée. She's the only one in the Universe who can *solve my issues.*"

"And it better stay that way, buster," I said with a giggle as I playfully slapped his perfect butt.

Gideon's manner grew serious. "Nothing short of death will ever change the way I love you. Even in death, my love for you won't end. That's my promise to you, Daisy."

My heart beat rapidly in my chest. I felt the same way. I had loved my first husband, Steve. He was a wonderful human being, but our marriage had been sadly flawed. He'd been my best friend and we'd grown into the adults we were together. His death had devastated me. His coming back as a ghost to make right what had been wrong for us gave him a special place in my heart forever. I'd thought I'd known true love. I hadn't... until the Grim Reaper came into my life.

Gideon was my soulmate. And I was his. Nothing short of death would separate us. I had no plans to die any time soon. I had way too much to live for.

"I feel sooo much better," I said as we walked out of our bedroom. "Thank you, Grim Reaper."

"Right back at you, Angel of Mercy slash Death Counselor," he replied with a grin. "You ready to kick some ass... fiancée?"

"Always, fiancé," I said with a giggle then raced him down the stairs.

A gaggle of ghosts were waiting in the living room, flying all over the place. It looked like Disney's Haunted Mansion on crack. I felt bad that I hadn't helped any of them lately, but they seemed content to stay for the moment. After my vacation, I'd dive back into my ghosts—so to speak.

"Dude," Heather said, waving ghosts away. "Get control of your people."

"Dead friends. Ease up," I called out. They hovered around me and waited. "Okay, here's the deal. I'm going to get Gram, Tory and Mr. Jackson. My family—chosen and blood—will stay here with you until I get back. I want you to be good, please. If a body part falls off, keep it with you. I'll glue it back on when I get home." I turned to Heather. "Can you make sure the Game Show Channel stays on while I'm gone?"

My sister gave me a thumbs up and handed me a burner phone and a slip of paper. "Will do. Tim has all the numbers recorded. This is a cheat sheet for you, just in case."

I gave her a quick hug and counted heads—Immortal and human. Everyone was here and ready.

"OH MY GOD!" Carl squealed, grabbing my left hand and holding it up for all to see. "Is this what I think it is?'

I blushed, nodded and smiled. Gideon just grinned like the cat who had bested the canary.

"Yes!" Heather yelled. "A wedding in our future. Best news ever."

Gideon and I were congratulated by all. Even my dead houseguests. Only Gabe was reserved. That was fine. His mind and energy were on Tory. I would have been the same if the situation was reversed. Candy Vargo offered to officiate. Gideon looked appalled at the suggestion. I was as well, but I'd learned never to discount or deny a gift. The overture was graciously accepted by me and not so graciously accepted by my fiancé.

"When's the wedding?" June asked, fussing over my ring.

"Not a clue," I admitted, admiring the gorgeous piece of

jewelry with her. "I just asked him to marry me a half hour ago."

"Badass," Candy said with a salute. "The baddest of the badasses."

I saluted the insane woman back. I'd take the compliment and continue to prove her right. I had to. Tory, Gram and Mr. Jackson's lives—or afterlives for Gram and Mr. Jackson—depended on it.

It was time to go to Kentucky.

THE AFTERNOON WAS SUNNY AND CHILLY. THE MAIL TRUCK trailed behind the minivan. Before we departed, there had been a brief debate about the queens bringing one of their horses, but Candy Vargo threatened not to give them boobs as their disguise if they pushed their luck. In the end twelve hours of a bouncy bosom outweighed the Horsemen wanting to bring a horse.

We were slated to arrive in Lexington, Kentucky shortly after midnight. Luckily, Jennifer's Airbnb was not rented out. Having someplace to stay without drawing attention to ourselves was excellent. We were definitely a motley crew. Tim had printed off maps and detailed photos of the castle in the hour we took to prepare. I'd memorized all of it during the first two hours of the drive. It was good to have something to focus on. Knowing the landscape was key. It kept me from worrying about Tory, Gram and Mr. Jackson.

"How much longer?" Candy bitched from the middle row of seats.

Gideon was driving. I rode shotgun. Gabe, Candy and Jennifer sat in the second row. Jolly Sue, Lura Belle and

Dimple were in the back. The Nephilim had been asleep for most of the trip so far. Gabe hadn't spoken a word. He'd studied the paperwork Tim had provided, then stared out of the window. Jennifer and Candy had played hangman on a pad of paper for two hours. Candy Vargo lost constantly. At one point, I thought she might blow up the vehicle. She also told Jennifer that the next time she won, she would hang her instead of the little stick guy. That didn't go over well. It had taken Gideon threatening to pull over and put Candy Vargo in the trunk to make her zip it and stop making ridiculous death threats.

"Four hours," I told her.

"I'm bored," she complained.

I rolled my eyes. She was worse than a kid.

"Not to worry," Jennifer announced. "I've got the remedy for that."

"No more hangman," I said quickly.

Jennifer cackled. "I value my dang life too much to play that again. We're gonna play a different car game."

"Gross facts?" Candy asked, perking up.

Jennifer shook her head. "Nope. It's called, Better Name For."

"Not following," I said, hoping this game wasn't going to make me want to hurl. Jennifer and Tim could clear a room with their knowledge of the nasty and unnecessary.

"Goes like this," she said, rubbing her little hands together with glee. "Someone comes up with a better name for an object and keeps it to themselves, then they ask everyone to try and guess the better name. Easy as pie."

From my experience, making pie was pretty freaking complicated, but I was willing to play along. "Sounds only slightly awful."

Jennifer cackled. "I'll go first. What's a better name for dentures?"

"Pain in the gums?" Jolly Sue called out from the back.

"Good one, but nope," Jennifer said with a giggle.

"Fake ass fuckin' chompers?" Candy guessed.

"Umm... no," Jennifer said. "Anyone else?"

"Porcelain pretenders?" Dimple tried.

"Ohhhhhh, that's excellent!" Jennifer congratulated her, reaching back and slapping Dimple a high five. "But that's not it."

Gideon usually didn't involve himself in the shenanigans, but the man couldn't help himself. "Fraudulent fangs?"

I laughed. The Grim Reaper had game.

"Holy cow! Jennifer shouted. "Damn good, but nope."

"We give up," I said.

She winked and handed out wine coolers. Gideon and Gabe both passed. "Dentures should be called substitooths!"

"Yessssss!" Lura Belle said. "Outstanding. I do believe I understand the activity. May I go next?"

"Be my guest," Jennifer insisted.

"Does it have to be something for people to guess, or may I make an astute observation?" Lura Belle inquired. "I'm not used to being included, so I don't want to mess it up."

Lura Belle's statement was sad but true. The old trio had been pariahs in our sleepy little Georgia town for decades. They'd deserved it. But today was a new day. The gals had changed and so had the rules. The thought made me smile. Sometimes truly good things occurred in life. The bad guys— or gals in this particular case—could be redeemed.

"Makin' the rules as we go," Jennifer assured her. "Go for it."

Lura Belle cleared her throat. "I believe that emotional baggage should be called a grief- case."

"What the actual fuck?" Candy Vargo shouted. "That was fuckin' profound."

"It was?" Lura Belle asked with delight.

"Damn straight," Candy said, offering the old woman a toothpick.

The energy had gone from bored and potentially violent to excited and silly.

"I've got one... I think," I said. "I believe that pick up artists and garbage men should swap titles."

"Word," Jennifer crowed. "Ain't that the truth!"

"Okiedokey," Candy Vargo announced. "I've got one."

We waited in terrified silence. She removed her toothpick then spoke. "Sexual tension should be re-termed bangxiety."

Even Gideon chuckled at that one. Candy preened and accepted high fives from all the gals in the minivan.

"A driveway should be a parkway and a parkway should be a driveway," Jennifer said.

"Bingo," I agreed. "And the snooze button on the alarm clock should be renamed five more minutes of denial."

"Winning! Daisy is winning!" Jolly Sue called out from the third row.

"Not so fuckin' fast," Candy argued. "Boob sweat should be called humidititties."

"I take it back," Jolly Sue said with a belly laugh. "Candy Vargo is winning!"

"I can't take this," Gideon muttered under his breath. "I have one."

"Spit it out, motherfucker," Candy encouraged him in the way only Candy could get away with.

"The term Dad Bod should henceforth be called Father Figure," he said with a twinkle in his eye.

"Gideon is winning!" Jolly Sue squealed. "I LOVE this game. Gabe, do you have one?"

All eyes went to the silent and brooding Gabe. My brother glanced back at Jolly Sue. Her smile was so wide and innocent, he sighed. "I don't think so."

"Oh, come on," Dimple said, patting his back. "You need to release the anger. It won't help you."

"Darn tootin'" Lura Belle agreed. "We know that for a fact. We've lived our whole lives as angry as bawdy, crook-plated hussies. Made for a yeasty barnacle of an existence. If you wanna be useful to Tory, you gotta ease up. You were not meant to be a dankish, mammering wagtail, Gabriel."

"Oh yes!" Dimple chimed in. "You're the Archangel Gabriel. You must stop behaving like a churlish, frothy giglet."

Jolly Sue nodded. "I quite agree with my sisters. If you want to defeat Micky Muggles, the bat-fowling, clack-dish imbecile, you must rise above your ire. Fury makes one sloppy and not very well liked... I speak from experience. If you truly love Tory, you must love her enough to be the man you are meant to be."

Again, Gabe sighed. He wasn't an angry man. He was a good and wonderful person. I adored my brother. The Nephilim were right, he needed to tamp back the fury in order to be any good to any of us.

Jennifer reached over and squeezed Gabe's hand. "It's easy. I promise. Just give it a try."

He looked down at her small hand in his and gave her a tight smile. "Fine. I shall oblige. A jet ski is an absurd name. It should be called a boatercycle."

"Gabe is winning!" Jolly Sue announced.

Gabe smiled his first real smile I'd seen since Tory was abducted.

"And one more," he said. "I believe that contractions should be called birthquakes."

The cheers in the car were loud. Gabe had definitely won, and I could attest to the truth of his last statement.

"And the championship wine cooler goes to Gabe," Jennifer announced, pulling out a bottle and presenting it to my brother. "You, sir, are the winner."

Gabe cracked it open, took a sip and winced. "What the hell is this?"

"Peach," Jennifer told him.

"Got it," he replied, taking another small sip and tried not to gag. "Thank you."

Candy Vargo clapped her hands. "I've got the final one. After that, we're gonna pull over 'cause I have to pee like a fuckin' race horse and pissing in the minivan isn't my idea of fun."

"Or mine," Jennifer said, scooting away from the Keeper of Fate.

"On it," Gideon said, pulling off the highway.

Candy Vargo crossed her legs and laid out a truth. "Love is like a fart. If you have to force it, it's most likely shit."

As gross as it was, it was profound—just like the woman herself.

I loved all the people in the minivan. No forcing necessary. Now, we just needed to save the others that we loved.

And we would.

CHAPTER FOUR

We rolled into Lexington, Kentucky at the expected time. Even though it was dark, the star-filled sky bathed the area in a magical silver glow. It was very pretty. Jennifer's Airbnb was on Second Street in the downtown area. The homes were stunning. We parked on the tree-lined street then made our way up the manicured stone walkway to the ornate front door.

"This should be called a fuckin' air-McMansion," Candy commented as we walked into Jennifer's Airbnb.

Candy wasn't wrong. I'd expected a cute little bungalow and that we'd be sleeping on couches and possibly the floor. Heck, I was prepared to sleep in the minivan. Not the case. It was a seven-bedroom Victorian house and it was lovely. Although, it was Victorian on the outside, it was all Jennifer on the inside—blindingly bright colors, comfortable furniture and a collection of ceramic ducks that defied logic.

"What the fuck with the ducks?" Candy asked, examining a group of fowl playing poker in the China cabinet.

My little human buddy guffawed. "I was wondering if anyone would mention the ducks."

"Kind of hard not to notice them," I told her with a grin.

"I think they're outstanding!" Tim said. "Did you know that female ducks choose their mate based on their dancing ability?"

"Bullshit," Candy said. "I used to lifeguard over at Woodson Park Lake twenty years back. I didn't see no dancing ducks."

"People don't swim at Woodson Park Lake," Dimple said, confused. "Why did they need a lifeguard?"

"Paddleboats. You wouldn't believe how many humans fall out of paddleboats." Candy snorted with disgust. "Never did have to get in the water and save no one, though. Just used to shout at them to get their asses back in the boats—scared the hell out of tons of drunk rednecks. But the real kicker... every damn morning, I had to scrub duck shit off them paddleboats. Fuckin' gross. Those feathered fucks had a whole park to take a crap in, but they crapped all over the paddleboats every night. In my opinion, ducks are rude-ass shittin' machines." She popped three toothpicks into her mouth and made herself comfortable on the couch. She wasn't done with her duck story yet. Leaning forward, she eyed us. I was positive we looked wildly unsure if we wanted her to keep going.

Keep going, she did... "One fine summer night after the park had closed, I sat outside on the dock with two bullhorns. Naked. Every time one of them flying fecal machines tried to take a dump on a paddleboat, I just blew the horns. They never saw it comin'. Ducks were flying around, bashing into each other and losing their tiny poop-lovin' minds. Those fuckers didn't shit on a single paddleboat that glorious night. Ended up getting arrested for disturbing the peace and indecent exposure. Good times."

Candy Vargo's stories were as batshit as she was. Everyone absorbed her tale in horrified silence.

"I'm very proud of you, Candy," Tim said.

We went from pondering Candy's insanity to confusion.

"Why are you proud of Candy?" I asked.

Tim smiled and patted Candy's head. "Normally, she'd incinerate the enemy. I find it wonderful she just deafened them."

"Thank you, Tim," she said.

"Welcome, friend."

"Such fascinating lives you lead," Wally commented. "I'll keep the naked bullhorn method in my Chanel pocketbook. But I must know the story of Jennifer's ducks! They're simply darling in a garish way."

"Craziest thing," Jennifer said, picking up a duck in a tiny hula skirt. Her smile was wistful. "My grandpappy—God rest his nutty soul—used to go to yard sales. He and his WWII veteran buds would scour yard sales, buy up a bunch of crap, then have their own yard sales. Absolutely insane!"

"Doesn't explain the ducks," Dirk pointed out, admiring a trio of ducks dressed in sequin skirts.

"Oh, but it does," she told him. "Grandpappy was kind of hard of hearin'. Used to call me up in college and shout into the phone every Sunday like clockwork. I'd answer him back, and when I was midsentence, he'd yell, 'Love ya, Baby' and hang up. That old geezer didn't hear a word I said. Loved him something fierce. One time he called me up and told me he got a great deal on some ducks. Said he was sending them. I told him no way in hell—I thought he meant real dang ducks! Anyhoo, he just yelled, 'Love ya, Baby' and hung up. That next week, I got eight big boxes filled with the ugliest ceramic ducks I'd ever seen."

"Oh my," Dimple said. "And you kept them?"

"All of 'em," Jennifer answered, kissing the head of a duck wearing rain boots and carrying an umbrella. "To me, they're the most beautiful ugly crap I own. Every single one is named, Baby in honor of my grandpappy—Hula Baby, Poker Baby, Sequin Baby, Salt and Pepper Baby. Kept them in the boxes until I got ownership of this house in my first divorce. Signed the paperwork for it on the very same date my grandpappy was born. Felt it was fitting to celebrate the hilarious old coot by displaying the ducks."

"Fierce!" Wally said. "I know your grandpappy is smiling down from the Light."

"Oh yesssssssss!" Fred exclaimed. "And this abode is to die for."

"You got it in your divorce?" Carl inquired.

"Yep," she confirmed. "Davis Braxton McNettles the Third —that cheating son of a bitch—was loaded. Trust fund loser," Jennifer commented wryly. "But even with a miniscule pecker, that asshole got around."

"Darling," Dirk said, checking himself out in the foyer mirror. "I'm surprised you married a man with a pocket-sized penis."

Jennifer shrugged. "Me too. But the microscopic shlong slinger made me laugh... until he didn't. Got married my junior year at UK. Stupid move, but hindsight is 20/20. That diminutive dick banged my entire sorority house. I was the last to know. He even banged the House Mother. She was seventy at the time. Live and learn." She chuckled as she looked around. "Took him to the cleaners. He deserved it."

"Well done," Lura Belle said, seating herself on the couch. "The egg-slinging, knotty-pated miscreant got what he deserved."

"Amen to that," Jennifer said. "Should I order up some food?"

I checked my watch. It was almost one in the morning. "No, it's really late. I think we should get some sleep."

"And when we wake up?" Gabe pressed, looking tense, but holding it together.

"We get our disguises on and take a tour of the place," I replied evenly.

"Solid," Candy Vargo announced, tucking a duck under her arm. "I have a plan to get the humans off the premises."

"The plan?" Gideon asked.

She eyed the Grim Reaper with a naughty smirk. "Questions are free. The answers might cost ya."

Gideon's eyes narrowed dangerously. The Keeper of Fate wasn't fazed.

"I'm not tellin'," she said with a wide grin.

"Oh my goodness," Tim said with a worried expression. "I don't like the sound of that."

Neither did I. I wondered if a bullhorn or being naked was involved. "No humans will die, correct?"

"No humans will die," she confirmed then walked out of the living room and up the stairs to find a bedroom to sleep in.

That was as good as it was going to get this evening. We'd find out what the Keeper of Fate had up her sleeve soon enough. I made a mental note for everyone to have earplugs on hand just in case.

"Jennifer, should we just find somewhere to sleep, or do you want to assign rooms?" I asked, yawning. I hadn't had a good night's sleep in a long time. Thankfully, Immortals could go quite a while without rest. But as a former human, I loved sleeping.

"Just go on up," she said, pointing to the stairs. "A few of the rooms have bunks and the others have king-sized beds. As long as y'all don't mind sharing, there should be plenty of room."

"Sounds like a plan, girlfriend," Dirk announced as he and the queens made their exit.

Tim, Gabe, Jennifer and the old gals followed them up.

"You ready for some shut-eye?" Gideon asked, taking my hand in his.

"So ready," I told him.

Right now, cuddling up to my gazillion-year-old fiancé and grabbing a few hours of rest sounded as good as the vacation I had planned.

One step at a time.

Sleep. Get disguised. Find out Candy Vargo's plan. Tour the Kentucky Castle. Take Micky Muggles out for good while saving Tory, Gram and Mr. Jackson.

It was a tall order, but I had no plan to lose.

I'D TAKEN THE LIBERTY OF SLEEPING IN UNTIL EIGHT. THE CASTLE wasn't open for tours until ten. Gideon grabbed a quick shower then slipped out to get coffee. It was difficult to get up. The bed was heavenly. However, sleeping wouldn't get Tory, Gram and Mr. Jackson back. And it definitely wouldn't bring about Micky Muggles' demise. After a shower and some clean sweats, I was ready to face the day.

"What the hell?" I muttered as I walked down the stairs and saw a room full of strangers eating donuts.

It didn't scare me. It was just unsettling. Although, most of my life since I had turned forty was unsettling…

"Taa-daa," Candy shouted, still looking like herself.

The rest of our crew... not so much. Ironically, I recognized everyone even though they looked nothing like they did last night. I could feel their essence. Lura Belle, Jolly Sue and Dimple were now teenage girls—somewhere between twelve and fifteen. Each wore jeans, brightly colored sweaters and tennis shoes. They were no longer sporting designer duds. They no longer had gray hair and sensible leather pumps. The three gals were grinning from ear to ear, admiring each other and gobbling down donuts.

Tim looked like a sweet old man around eighty. He wore chinos, a button-down with a cardigan and sensible shoes. Normally, he was forty-ish and always dressed in his mail uniform. Immortals could choose their age. Most of them that I'd come across chose upper thirties to early fifties. My real age was forty, and I'd felt every year of it lately.

Jennifer was the counterpart to Tim—eighty-ish and adorable. In real life, my buddy was sixty-five and had over-Botoxed her face until you couldn't tell if she was pissed or happy. Her new beau, the kind and wonderful Sheriff Dip Doody, had convinced her to stop all that crap. She didn't need it. She was beautiful without chemical help. Today, she was full of wrinkles and had a nice neat gray bun at the nape of her neck. Her house dress was a colorful muumuu and of course, she wore sensible shoes.

Gabe, who was normally drop-dead handsome, could have easily gotten lost in a crowd. Last night, he was tall, blond and gorgeous. Right now, he was short with dull brown hair and a mustache. He wore jeans, work boots and a plain beige flannel shirt. He paced the room and kept glancing at his watch. My brother was raring to go.

Everyone so far seemed fine with their new visages. Dirk, Wally, Fred and Carl were *very* happy.

The queens were flipping their shit. All four of the
Horsemen were now women—quite attractive ladies around
forty. They were clad in trendy, yet understated preppy outfits.
They wore soccer-mom hairdos and subtle makeup. While the
look was slightly alarming due to being used to their over-the-
top flamboyance, it was nothing compared to what they were
doing.

All four had their hands on their boobs and were squeezing
with unabashed delight. Wally cried tears of joy. Fred—in
between squeezes—bounced up and down in front of the foyer
mirror. Carl circled the room muttering the word boobs over
and over. Dirk had stripped down to his bra and shimmied,
making his newly found C-cups come dangerously close to
exiting his undergarment.

"Umm... guys," I said in my outdoor voice to break through
the boob frenzy. "Get the knocker fondling out of your system.
That behavior isn't going to fly in public"

They heeded my advice and groped themselves with
urgency. It was both funny and disturbing. Whatever. Our lives
were dangerous. Our survival unsure. We'd all clearly learned
to grab some happiness where we could get it. The Four
Horsemen of the Apocalypse just grabbed with a little more
gusto than the rest.

I turned to face the love of my life. He looked disgruntled,
and it was all I could do not to laugh.

Gideon, who appeared to be around fifty, was dumpy and
very nondescript. His shirt was tucked into his pants, revealing
a gut. My Greek God of a partner had let himself go—or
rather, Candy had let him go. The Grim Reaper was sporting a
Dad Bod, or Father Figure, to be more accurate. His normally
thick blond hair was dishwater brown and receding. It was

bizarre. Strangely, I was still attracted to dumpy, hair-challenged Gideon.

"Dude," I said with a laugh as I looked him up and down. "Hot."

He rolled his eyes and handed me a coffee. "I'll get Candy Vargo back for this eventually."

I had no doubt he would. Payback was a bitch.

"I'm ready for my disguise," I told Candy.

She gave me a thumbs up and handed me a toothpick. "I figured you'd be the mom to the dumb-dumbs and Gideon is the dad."

"Who does that make everyone else?" I asked, scared of what she was about to make me look like.

"Don't matter," she replied. "We're too many people. I suggest that the fuckin' titty ticklin' crew stay here and protect Jennifer. We've got maps and we know where we're goin'. Plus, it don't look like they're gonna stop twistin' their tatas for a good long while."

I spared a quick glance at the queens. They were still going to town. Candy had made a good point.

"I agree with that," Tim chimed in. "I shall ride with you to the castle, but stay in the minivan. I've rigged it with satellite Wi-Fi so I can do any research or get in touch with backup if we need it."

"I like the way you think, mailman," Candy told him. "Gabe and I will pose as a couple."

Gabe winced and closed his eyes. His relationship with Candy was kind of iffy. He, Prue, Abby and Rafe had been eaten by Candy centuries ago. Granted, they'd tried to destroy her on Zadkiel's dastardly orders, and she'd apparently done what she had to do, being that she had been legless and armless at the time. To this day, I couldn't comprehend how my siblings were actually alive. The logistics were mind-boggling and stomach-churning. Part of me itched to ask the particulars, but my sense of self-preservation and my dislike of throwing up stopped me. Some things were better left unsaid.

Gabe finally spoke. His voice was tight, and the tone was flat. "Fine. Will Tory recognize me?"

"Yeah," Candy said. "She might not recognize the rest of us, but she will know you no matter the visage."

Gabe gave her a curt nod of thanks.

I looked at my watch. "Tim, how long will it take us to get to the castle by car?"

"Half hour," he replied.

"Great," I said, picking up the glazed donut and taking a bite. It wasn't the breakfast of champions, but something in my stomach was better than nothing. "We'll leave in twenty minutes."

Dirk stepped forward and curtseyed to Candy Vargo. "I would like to thank you for my sweater meat, doll face," he said. "My lady-nuts are indeed luscious."

"And my chesticles are charming," Wally announced, bowing deeply to the Keeper of Fate. "Although it will only be but twelve hours of possessing sweater stretchers, I will cherish every moment."

"Y'all are fuckin' crazy," Candy Vargo muttered with a chuckle.

"My gozangas are both glorious and gorgeous," Carl announced. "For this limited gift, I shall grant you horseback riding lessons on my steed."

Everyone in the room gasped. No one rode the steeds of the Four Horsemen of the Apocalypse except the Four Horsemen of the Apocalypse.

"Oh my," Tim said, shocked and impressed. "Is that allowed?"

Carl shrugged and felt himself up. "Probably not, but one profound gift deserves another."

Fred joined the conversation. "I say it's fine, although, we should probably chat with the steeds first. They can be quite temperamental beasts. However, that being said, my beefy magambos are a blessing. Falsies are wonderful, but there's nothing like the real thing, baby! Thank you, Candy Vargo. In addition to you possibly dying atop Carl's steed, I'd like to supply you with toothpicks for the rest of your existence— which might be cut short due to the horseback riding."

"Okay, fuckers," Candy said with an eye roll. "I ain't ridin' your damned horses, but I'll gladly accept the toothpicks."

We were a motley crew about to venture into the unknown. I'd been in battles—deadly battles, but no humans had been involved. What we were about to do made me feel way off-center. The Immortals I loved were very cognizant and respectful of human life. I was beginning to think that my friends might be an exception to the rule. Immortal law stated that human life was sacred and not to be extinguished. However, Micky Muggles didn't adhere to Immortal law.

He wasn't Immortal.

He wanted to be, but that wasn't going to happen.

Candy waved her hand. In the blink of an eye, I went from an attractive forty-year-old woman to a decade older not-so-hot middle-aged gal with a bowl cut and an ugly prairie-looking frock. My formerly curly dark long hair was peppered with gray, and my shoes were something I wouldn't wish on my worst enemy. To add salt to the wound, they weren't even comfortable.

"Seriously?" I asked, looking at myself in the foyer mirror with dismay. "You could've at least made the shoes orthopedic."

"Cakehole. Shut it," Candy Vargo said as she waved her hand again and disguised herself.

I almost choked on my spit when she transformed. I looked bad, but she was a hot mess.

The Keeper of Fate was an attractive woman. Granted, she was messy and dressed like she'd found her wardrobe in a dumpster, but she'd chosen a look that beat her sloppy one hands down. Candy now appeared to be around forty and looked like she'd lived hard. Her skin was sun damaged, and the lines on her face were deep. Her mom-jeans were floods, and her sweater was too tight, revealing a gut that made Gideon's look like a little pooch. The kicker? She was missing her front tooth.

"Oh my God," Gabe's brow shot up as he choked on a laugh. "Sexy," he deadpanned.

The group of us chuckled, and I was glad to see that my brother wasn't so consumed by his rage that he'd lost all sense of humor.

"Fuck you," Candy Vargo shot back with a grunt of amusement. "We can all blend into a crowd now without being noticed."

"I'm going to have to disagree," Tim said, examining Candy's mouth with curiosity. "The missing tooth is rather out there."

She rolled her eyes and waved her hand. All of her teeth had returned, but they were dark gray. "Better?"

"Nope," I said with an eye roll. "Fix your damn mouth."

"Y'all ain't no fun," she muttered, taking my advice. Also, my shoes were suddenly more comfortable, proving once again that the Keeper of Fate wasn't always an asshole.

"We're not here to have a good time," Gideon reminded her in a flat tone.

"Speak for yourself," she said. "I'm gonna enjoy the hell out of watching Micky Muggles go down in flames. I'm itchin' for a juicy justice boner."

"Enough," I said, checking the time and tucking my burner phone into the pocket of my heinous dress. "It's time to go."

The atmosphere in the room went from light to heavy.

Dirk stepped forward, his hands sill on his breasts. He looked silly, but his words were not. "In your search for something positive, look around the corners—surprises often lurk there. Sometimes one might dream of never being called strong again. They might be exhausted by their strength. One might want a break from the madness. They long for understanding and not to be admired for how well they take a hit or how often. However, according to Marcus Aurelius, 'You have the power over your mind—not outside events. Realize this, and you will find strength.'"

I pressed my lips together and nodded. He had spoken words I needed to hear. Yes, my life had been a rollercoaster of trying to stay alive, but I had so much to live for. I was going to ride it until it came to a stop.

The Horsemen weren't done with their sage advice.

Carl joined Dirk. His hands were also glued to his bosom, but his expression was somber. "Charles Dickens said, 'There are dark shadows on the earth, but its lights are stronger in contrast.'" Carl adjusted his breasts and gave me a kiss on the cheek. "With great power comes even greater responsibility, girlfriend. Immortality is a tricky game. However, you must remember that out of our greatest battles come miracles. Keep that in mind when you think you have no more to give."

Again, I nodded. Guilt swept over me for wanting a break.

Lives of people I loved were on the line. Being tired was no excuse. Gideon had said there had been centuries where nothing bad had happened. I'd experience that too... eventually. Adjusting my expectations was the answer. I was at the very beginning of Immortality. To fathom living forever was impossible and a waste of time I didn't have. What I did have was a daughter I would happily die for—like my own mother had done for me. My friends and family were more valuable to me than all the riches in existence. And, finally, there was Gideon, my other half, my love and my fiancé. A small smile pulled at my lips. Yes, my life had dark shadows, but the lights were glorious in contrast. Charles Dickens was a profound man.

It was Wally's turn. I listened to every word. The queens were saving my ass. They knew it and I knew it. I loved the breast-obsessed boys with my whole heart.

"I shall start with a quote," Wally said, patting his boobs lovingly. "The very astute Thomas A. Edison said, 'When you have exhausted all the possibilities, remember this: you haven't.' And the illustrious Candy Vargo coined a term that I shall keep in my vocabulary."

"Fuckin' fuckers?" Candy asked.

Wally closed his eyes for a brief moment then sighed dramatically. "Umm... no. It was the term, juicy justice boner. That's the goal. The orgasmic results will be worth it."

"Ahh... okay," I said. "Thank you."

Wally bowed to me as Fred stepped up with a grip on his breasts that looked as painful as my last mammogram. I didn't comment.

"My darling," Fred began. "The charming Mahatma Ghandi once said, 'Strength does not come from physical capacity. It comes from indomitable will.' Now with that being said, you do indeed have physical capacity. Your power is beyond what I have experienced in all my many, many, many years. However, it's your will that must stay strong. That's the key. And I too agree that a *juicy justice boner* is an exciting way to look at the big picture."

Dirk patted my bowl cut and smiled. "Use what you know. Aid always comes from unexpected places."

Their words gave me strength. I wasn't alone. My small army consisted of some of the most powerful Immortals alive —the Grim Reaper, the Archangel Gabriel, the Immortal Courier, the Keeper of Fate and myself. Jolly Sue, Lura Belle and Dimple were Nephilim, but they'd been given an extra boost by my Angel siblings. Our backup was the Four Horsemen of the Apocalypse. We were a badass team.

There was still some business to get done here.

"Jennifer," I said, hugging my friend. "First off, thank you for your hospitality. I love you. Secondly, do you happen to have any superglue? I don't know what state I'll find Gram and Mr. Jackson in, and I'd like to be prepared."

"Sure do," she said with a grin. "June put a few tubes in my purse just in case!"

Jennifer handed the glue tubes over, and I tucked them into my pockets.

"Questions for Candy," I said, turning to the Immortal. "Can you remove the disguises if necessary?"

"Yep," she confirmed. "Just give me the word and they're gone."

"Good," I said, pacing the living room and adjusting my attitude. I thought better when I moved. "Out of curiosity, is there any way to actually make Micky Muggles Immortal?"

"Please don't tell me you would do that," Tim said wringing his hands.

"I didn't say I would do it. I asked if it was possible," I replied evenly. Granting the cretin immortality was a very bad idea. I knew that. However, Gram, Tory and Mr. Jackson's lives were more important than making a terrible decision.

Gideon answered. "No. It's not possible. However, I don't think it's wise to let him know. Until Tory, Gram and Mr. Jackson are safe, I believe it's prudent that the imbecile believes it can happen."

Gabe growled. It sent a chill skittering up my spine. "If it was possible, I'd do it to save Tory. I'd then spend the rest of my days tracking him down to decapitate him. Make no mistake... I would find him, and I'd make his death slow and excruciatingly painful."

"Mmmkay," Dimple said with an uncomfortable giggle. "I believe we've gotten a bit off track. The gorbellied, malt-worm clack-dish isn't worth this debate. His demise is coming shortly. That's the plan. It would be an honor to save the day and destroy the cockerd hussy."

"I quite agree," Lura Belle chimed in. "And please don't forget that in a pinch, my sisters and I are more than willing to use our teeth as weapons to remove the penis where the yeasty barnacle's power is stored."

"More than willing is a bit of a stretch," Jolly Sue pointed out as she ducked the wild punch Lura Belle threw her way. "BUT, if we have too, we will."

They looked like teens. The words coming out of their mouths were crazy peppered with language from the fifteenth century. Life was upside down. However, they'd made some good observations. We simply needed to focus on the end game.

A thought came to me, and I acted on it. "New safe word.

We can't risk that Micky Muggles didn't get it out of Tory, Gram or Mr. Jackson."

"What do you want it to be?" Gideon asked.

I smiled. It was a no-brainer. "Juicy justice boner."

My soulmate's eyes grew wide for only a brief second, then he chuckled. "Juicy justice boner it is."

Gabe walked over to me and touched my cheek. "I'm humbled by you, sister. You have my word that I will contain my fury and fight by your side. You're someone I aspire to emulate. However, please keep in mind that Tory, Gram and Mr. Jackson still believe the safe word to be toothpick."

I placed my hand over my brother's and smiled. "Correct and thank you. We'll get them back. That's the main goal. Period. If Micky Muggles gets away, so be it. We'll deal with him eventually." I looked around. The energy was electric. "We ready?"

The chorus of yesses was expected. We were out for a juicy justice boner, and we were going to get it.

CHAPTER FIVE

THE RIDE TO KENTUCKY CASTLE HAD BEEN PRETTY.
Lexington's landscape was full of rolling hills and impressive
horse farms. The air held a winter chill much colder than
Georgia, but Candy Vargo provided everyone with warm
coats. The tension in the minivan was palpable. No one had
much to say. Not surprising since we had no clue what we
were about to walk into. As before, Gideon drove, and I rode
shotgun. Tim sat in the second row with Candy and Gabe. The
Nephilim were in the back.

As we pulled up the long drive to the castle, my brow wrinkled in confusion. Something wasn't right. In fact, it was very
wrong. My stomach tightened and my fingers tingled. I
tamped back my magical distress. It would be bad form to
blow up the minivan with all of us sitting in it.

"Pull in behind the tree line to give us cover," I instructed
Gideon.

"Already on it," he replied, expertly maneuvering the
minivan to a hidden spot. We could see the structure in front
of us, but we were mostly obscured from view.

"Are you sure the pictures you gave us were correct?" I asked Tim, squinting at the massive Tudor buildings. It didn't look remotely like it was supposed to.

"Yes," Tim said, frantically typing on his laptop. "Well, shit. Shit, shit, shit."

I'd never heard Tim cuss in the entire time I'd known him. It didn't bode well.

"It's familiar to me," Gideon said, squinting at the array of buildings. "Has anyone seen it before?"

Candy leaned forward. "Fuck me running" she said. "Looks like we took a wrong turn somewhere. That right there in front of us is the Tower of London."

Pressing my lips together so I didn't scream, I cracked my knuckles and willed myself to stay calm. For the moment, I'd search for facts. Magic wasn't factual, but there was always truth in what most perceived to be fiction. "Tim, check the GPS. Are we in London, England or Lexington, Kentucky?"

"Lexington, Kentucky," he confirmed. "However, until you get inside the fortress, we can't be sure."

Gideon inhaled deeply and gripped the steering wheel so tight his knuckles turned white. "How does that bastard have so much power?" he ground out with his eyes turning a bright and furious red. "He's a fucking Nephilim."

"Hopped up on Immortal blood," Gabe reminded everyone.

"He has to be running out," Tim said without thinking. He winced as Gabe punched the passenger window so hard his fist went through it.

No one chastised my brother. It was better than him blowing something up. Announcing our arrival was the last thing we wanted to do.

Candy Vargo rolled down the window and sniffed the air. "Fucker's so powerful cause he ain't workin' alone."

I watched as a group of people entered the compound. There was a pep in their steps that made me grind my teeth.

"You wanna be more specific?" I demanded of Candy. This was a twist I wasn't expecting.

"Can't," she said. "I need to get in there to tell what's goin' on."

"Nephilim," Lura Belle called out from the back as she shuddered. "I can feel the presence of many Nephilim."

I looked over at Gideon. "Is that a bad thing, a good thing or a disastrous thing?"

He shrugged and cut the engine. "Only one way to find out."

Candy Vargo exited the minivan and sniffed the air again. "I got good news and bad news. What do ya want first?"

"Good news," I said as we joined her on the lawn, but still hidden behind the tree line.

"Ain't no humans in there."

I heaved a sigh of relief. "Bad news?"

She pulled out a toothpick and jammed it into her mouth. "I detect about a hundred others."

"All Nephilim?"

She shook her head. "Nope. A gut-punch combo of Demons, Nephilim and a few Angels thrown into the mix."

Tim stepped out of the car and stared at the replica of the Tower of London. At least, I hoped it was a replica. If that bastard had enough power to plop a chunk of England into the middle of Kentucky... I shook my head. That nightmare-scenario was too terrible to entertain.

"My guess is the word is out that Micky Muggles is going to be granted Immortality," Tim said. "That would be something many would want to observe."

I shook my head in disbelief. "Aren't they all aware that's impossible?"

My mailman buddy pinned me with a gaze. "Micky seems to have borrowed our motto—everything is possible, you just have to believe."

"He's shit out of luck on that one," I snapped. While our motto was inspiring and had gotten me through a lot, it wasn't bulletproof. If it was, my mom would still be here. My dad too. They were not.

And Micky Muggles wasn't going to be here much longer if I had anything to do with it.

"This is not good," Lura Belle said, fretting. "King Henry the Eighth lived here. This is where he beheaded Anne Boleyn. Not good. Not good at all."

"I don't like this one little bit," Jolly Sue muttered. "The haggard, fat-kidneyed, nut hook fancies himself a reincarnation of Henry the Eighth."

Pressing the bridge of my nose, I made myself stay on task. Freaking out would help no one. In the past the missions had seemed obvious. This one didn't. It made me itchy and unsure. The feeling was awful. "The plan at this point is to enter the premises and figure out what the hell is going on."

"Split or stay together?" Gabe asked.

I looked at my friends. "Candy and Gabe stick together. The Nephilim will stay with Gideon and myself. Tim, stay back and keep gathering information. Focus on King Henry, please. We'll take one hour to poke around, chat with people if you can then meet back at the entrance."

"Do we know each other?" Candy Vargo asked, looking wildly excited.

I glanced over at Gideon. He shrugged. "My guess is that we'll recognize some within the walls. Immortals live for a long time. Many know each other. I'd say keep our interactions polite, but not too familiar."

"One more thing," I said to Candy. "Can you do something so our power is muted, and our presence isn't a dead giveaway? With some extra stress on the word dead."

"Nope, but the Grim Reaper can," she replied pointing at Gideon.

"Good thinking," he said. Gideon snapped his fingers and produced a razor-sharp dagger. Without hesitation, he sliced a deep gash into his palm. I gasped as the blood gushed from his hand, but he didn't even flinch. The love of my life chanted quietly in a language I'd heard him use before. It was melodic and I didn't understand a word. As the air warmed around us, blood red sparks began to dance on his wounded palm. He raised his arm into the air then slashed it down to his side. The spell hit me like a punch to the gut. I went down along with Jolly Sue, Lura Belle and Dimple like a sack of potatoes. Candy, Tim, Gabe and Gideon were still standing.

Cautiously getting to my feet, I checked to make sure there wasn't a huge gaping hole where my stomach used to be. Nope. I was fine and so were the Nephilim.

"My goodness," Dimple said, shaking the dirt off her jeans. "That was unexpected."

"No pain, no gain as I always say," Lura Belle grunted as she got up and pulled Jolly Sue to her feet.

"It's time," Gabe said, raring to get inside.

"One thing to remember," Tim commented as he got back into the minivan and opened his laptop. "When magic is being used to create illusions, time runs differently. I'd suggest you work with measured and controlled urgency. A human week might not apply once you are in."

That sucked. "How will we know?"

"We won't," Gideon replied, tucking the dagger into his sock and covering it with his pant leg. "We'll just work on the assumption that time is of the essence."

"Gather all the info you can," I told the group as we calmly walked toward the entrance. "Nothing you hear is unimportant."

"Roger that," Candy Vargo said as she grabbed Gabe's hand.

To his credit, he didn't deck her. Putting them together might be a mistake, but it was Candy's suggestion. The Keeper of Fate was rarely wrong. I wasn't going to mess with whatever she had planned.

While fate was fickle and could change on a dime, it was all we had to go on right now. Micky Muggles' goal of immortality was not possible. However, my goal was.

Anything was possible as long as I believed. I believed I would win and would accept nothing less.

CHAPTER SIX

TO ENTER WE WALKED OVER A BRIDGE THAT HAD CLEARLY crossed a large moat at one time. There was no water beneath us, just grass. The structures inside were imposing, and I wished I had studied history a little better. That was on my list of things to do, along with reading the Bible. It was a good thing I was Immortal. My list got longer every day. I knew that Anne Boleyn had been decapitated here, but little else. There was a feeling of menace in the compound along with morbid fascination. I had a gut feeling that Tim's guess about Micky Muggles bragging about becoming Immortal had been correct.

The masses would be disappointed.

No one batted an eye as we walked around. Our disguises made us blend seamlessly and go unnoticed. After we'd made it in, Candy and Gabe turned left and we turned right. It looked nothing like the castle in Lexington, Kentucky we'd prepared ourselves for. It was ancient, weathered and gave off tremendously bad juju.

I noticed ghosts everywhere, but they weren't similar to the dead guests that came to me for aid. I guesstimated at least thirty to forty. Specters were difficult to count since they wove in and out of each other. The dead here were skittish, scared and badly decomposing. They were curious about me and began to follow us. That wouldn't help me stay undercover. My heart and loyalty to my job as the Death Counselor urged me to do something for them, but that would have to wait. However, I did wonder if they had any helpful information.

"Cover me for a sec," I told Gideon and the gals.

They surrounded me without question. Hidden from the view of any casual bystanders, I squatted low and covertly gestured to one of the dead to come close. He hesitated before zipping down and hovering in front of me.

"I'm Daisy," I whispered with a kind smile.

"Graaaaagraunchah," he replied, eyeing me with hope, excitement, and a good dose of fear.

The ghost had seen better days. He was falling apart. It took all I had not to pull out the superglue and repair him a little, but there was no time right now.

"It's nice to meet you. I'm not here to hurt you," I told him, gently touching his decayed face. "I'm the Death Counselor. I'm trying to save two ghosts and an Immortal friend who were kidnapped by Micky Muggles. Do you know of any new ghosts here?"

"Yesssssssah," he said as he quivered and swayed in the light wind.

"Where? Where are they?" My heart pounded in my chest. Could it be this easy? Could we simply find Gram, Mr. Jackson and Tory and whisk them out of this hell on earth?

"Doooontha knooooowah," he told me.

It was not going to be easy. Nothing was easy.

I smiled again even though it took some effort. "I promise to help you and the others after I've accomplished what I came here to do. I need you and the rest of the dead not to follow too closely. It will let the bad guy know I'm here. Do you understand?"

"Yesssssssah," he said. "Graaaaagraunchah willllllllllll obeeeeyah."

"Thank you, umm... Gragraunch. If you learn anything about the two new ghosts, please come and find me."

He floated back to the others. I stood up and squeezed Gideon's hand. We continued to explore and observe for at least ten minutes to make sure our disguises were solid before we approached anyone.

"It looks like way more than a hundred people," I whispered to Gideon as we walked down the cobblestone path.

He nodded curtly and took Jolly Sue and Dimple's hands. I grabbed Lura Belle's and led us over to a bench where others were chatting. As soon as the milling people saw us approach the occupants of the bench, the path cleared lickety-split and we were no longer in a crowd. It was interesting and unnerving. The only people left were us and a quartet of beefy looking Immortal idiots.

We were sized up immediately by four rather seedy male Demons and discounted as unimportant. Tamping back our power had been a good move. We seemed irrelevant in the power structure.

"Hi there," I said, waving at the largest of the Demons. "Nice day!"

Gideon's eyes had narrowed dangerously, and he glanced down to hide his expression. My guess was that he knew them or, at least, of them. I proceeded with caution.

The Demon's brows raised in annoyance. "Did you actually speak to me? You're not worthy to be in my presence. Be gone, scum."

Slapping myself in the forehead, I giggled with fake embarrassment. "I'm so sorry. We've just come such a long way to see the dragon become Immortal, I was hoping someone could tell us when the festivities begin. You four look so strong and capable, I assumed you were in charge. My bad. Come on, friends, we'll find someone more important along the way."

I ushered the gals and Gideon to follow.

"Not so fast," a shorter Demon snarled, stepping in front of me. His feral grin was as sickly as his body odor. The stench of sulfur was real. It was all I could do not to hold my nose or gag. He glanced around to make sure no one else was nearby. The area was deserted, and he believed he had the upper hand.

He was about to fuck around and find out.

"You're not a Demon," he said monotone as he poked my shoulder with a thick finger and threw me off balance. "Can't figure out what you are. I don't like it when I can't figure it out. Makes me wanna kill something. You know what I mean, lady? You got a nice neck. Sure would love to snap it."

His cohorts laughed. I joined them. They were a little confused.

I crossed my fingers and prayed that Gideon wouldn't lose his shit. I could take care of myself if need be. The stinky asshole invading my space would be dust in two seconds if I chose to end him.

"I can't figure out what I am either!" I laughed like I'd just made the funniest joke in the world. Honestly, we just needed to get out of here. They were not going to be of help and blowing our cover after being here for only fifteen minutes wasn't a good plan of action. "It's just nutty. Well, sorry to bother you. We'll leave you be."

They sneered and looked me up and down. My little family

of five was now surrounded by odiferous asswipes, who had no clue who they were messing with.

"You have money, bitch?" a third asked with a leer on his face. "Or maybe you'd like to sell one of your Nephilim? I could do with a little half-Angel, half-human poon right now. Little sex. Little death."

"You got that right, buddy," the big guy said with a grin that made my stomach churn. "I'd suggest you move along and leave the Nephilim here. If that doesn't work for you, we can kill you and your guy first. Either way, we get the Nephilim. Capiche?"

Jolly Sue, Lura Belle and Dimple quickly moved to Gideon. I could tell he was about to go Grim Reaper on their ugly asses. This was going south fast. I shoved my sparking hands into my pockets. I scanned the area for other Immortals. None, thank, Heavens. I practically squealed with relief.

The Demons were repulsive and stupid. If they made another move toward the sisters, they wouldn't live to make another lurid remark.

As if by silent agreement, the bigger of the assholes, shoved me into a stone wall, and the others lunged for the girls.

Playtime was over.

"Keep them safe," I said to Gideon as the demon pressed my cheek against the cold stone. I was itching for some retribution. I knocked the jerk holding me back several feet, pleased with the look of surprise coloring his expression. I gave him my own feral grin and winked at Gideon. "I'll take care of these stank-breath idiots."

"My pleasure," he replied in a venomous tone that gave the Demons pause.

I made a come-at-me-bro gesture, my grin never wavering.

Silly Demons didn't stop long enough to wonder why I

wasn't afraid of them. Instead, like the raging idiots they were, they came at me like derailed freight trains on a crash course into the Darkness. It seemed they were in the mood to die. In less time than it took to blink, three of them were dust at my feet. All it had taken was a clap of my now flaming hands. The remaining dickhead tried to run.

He was out of luck.

Gideon was on him so fast I barely saw the Grim Reaper move. My other half shoved the waste of space into a dark alcove. He put his knee on the disgusting Demon's chest and his hands around the dude's throat. The Demon's eyes were bugging with shock and fear.

Jolly Sue, Lura Belle and Dimple stood watch as I approached the simpering fool who'd tried to harm my people.

"Name," I ground out as Gideon held him down with ease.

"Who are you?" he demanded of both of us.

"Not important," I snapped. "Give me your name."

Gideon hissed and squeezed the Demon's neck harder. "His name is Ragon. He's wanted by the Goddess of the Darkness for deeds so heinous and repulsive I hesitate to speak them aloud. I say we deliver him to her... in pieces."

"Hmm..." I smiled coldly at the now very fearful Demon. "Not sure how that would work. If I remove his appendages and beat him senseless before I decapitate him, wouldn't all of his parts turn to dust before they arrived to the Goddess of Darkness?"

"Interesting," Gideon said in a polite and conversational tone. "Fine point. Well made."

The Demon paled considerably. "I'll tell you anything," he choked out since his airway was being crushed by Gideon. "Anything you want to know."

"Isn't that sweet," I said, squatting down and getting as close to his face as I could without gagging on his breath. "Aren't you the one who wanted some Nephilim poon?"

"Didn't mean it," he swore. "Just messing with you."

"Really?" I asked. "And the attempted murder was a joke too?"

He didn't have an answer to that. However, if he was willing to chat before he left this realm for good, I was all ears.

"He's committed crimes against women and children," Gideon mind-spoke to me with red-hot fury in his voice. *"He's wanted and will be put to death immediately. I'm going to kill him unless you would like the honors. It will save my sister some time and she'll owe me."*

"His punishment can come from you. The less I have to do with the Goddess of Darkness, the better," I told him.

The Grim Reaper gave me a curt nod.

"Here's the deal," I said, winking at Ragon which caused him to whimper. "You're going to die. Sorry not sorry about that. People who harm children and women don't deserve to breathe. So here's how I see it. If you'd like to do one good deed in your slimy life before it's lights out time, you'll tell us what's going on here. If you'd prefer not to, that's fine."

"What's in it for me?" he growled.

"A quick, easy death or a quick, painful one," I replied flatly. We didn't have time for the slow death he deserved, but we could definitely make it excruciating.

The Demon mulled it over. When he noticed the red sparks flying from Gideon's eyes, he started talking. "The Dragon King will be given Immortality by the Angel of Mercy," he admitted.

"Not possible," I shot back.

"It's true," he insisted desperately.

I was already aware of that part. I wanted something I didn't know. "When?"

"Sometime after the sacrifice," he replied. "He plans to behead Anne Boleyn in an hour."

I rolled my eyes, blew out a long breath and glanced over my shoulder to make sure the coast was still clear. It was. "Anne Boleyn is already dead."

"Fuck you," he spat. "It's all I know."

I looked at Gideon. "He held up his end. Quick death it is." I narrowed my gaze at our captive. "But make it painful."

"But I told you everything I know," the Demon cried. "You said I'd get a quick, easy death!"

"Oh," I nodded slyly. "It will be as easy as pie, and not even an iota of what you deserve."

"Good riddance to bad rubbish," Gideon said tonelessly. "Compliments of the Grim Reaper,"

Rogan's eyes widened as terror filled his gaze. "The Grim—"

Without flourish or fanfare, the Grim Reaper cut Rogan off mid-sentence by ripping his head clean from his body. Within seconds, he was dust.

I shuddered thinking about all his victims and what he might've done to them. "Did you make it hurt?"

"Baby, I promise you, he's still feeling it," Gideon assured me.

I nodded my approval. "Good."

My guy stood up and waved his hands. The remains of all four Demons blew away in the wind. They would not be missed.

"Oh my goodness," Dimple said. "That was violent."

I tilted my head and squinted at her. "You bit the ass off of Micky Muggles."

"Forgot about that," she replied with a giggle. "Thank you, Gideon and Daisy, for saving us. The favor shall be repaid."

"No need," Gideon said. "If memory serves me right, the spot where Anne Boleyn was beheaded is up the hill."

"Do we have time to check it out, or do we need to meet up with Candy and Gabe at the entrance?" I asked.

Gideon pointed up the cobblestone path. The Keeper of Fate and the Archangel were headed our way. "No need. We will stay together as a group. It's far too dangerous here."

That was something I agreed with. While Gideon, Candy, Gabe and I could defend ourselves, the Nephilim would be toast against an evil Immortal. I hoped we hadn't made a grave mistake by letting them come with us.

Gabe got right down to it. His question was to the Nephilim. "Do you feel Micky Muggles presence?"

They shook their heads.

The Archangel's frustration was evident. I didn't blame him, but it wasn't going to help.

"He's here somewhere," I assured him. "He's supposed to behead Anne Boleyn in an hour."

"What the actual fuck?" Candy muttered. "She's already dead."

Jolly Sue raised her hand. I nodded to her.

"Is reincarnation possible?" she asked.

I didn't have an answer for that one.

"I mean, is it possible that the pribbling, weedy hedge-pig is truly the reincarnation of King Henry the Eighth?"

"Nope," Candy Vargo stated flatly. "That fucker, Micky Muggles, has been alive for too long."

My mind raced with questions. "Is reincarnation possible?"

Gabe took the lead. "It has been heard of, but I have no proof. As the tale goes, if someone dies before their time or under suspect and illegal circumstances, they have a chance to come back."

Gideon appeared doubtful. Candy Vargo just scratched her head with a toothpick. Gabe's tale was more of a non-answer—more like folklore.

"If I had to call it," Candy said. "My guess is that it's all an act. Maybe, that brainless fuck cast Tory as Anne Boleyn."

"No," Gideon said quickly as Gabe looked on the verge of a blow up. "He needs her to get Immortality from Daisy. He's stupid, but not that stupid. I'd say he's going to behead a random woman."

"Not on my watch," I said and began marching up the hill in the direction that Gideon had pointed earlier.

My crew followed behind me. This was a puzzle that kept getting uglier.

Dirk's advice danced in my mind. *Use what you know. Aid always comes from unexpected places.* I'd already heeded the tip. I wasn't sure it would come to much, but reaching out to the dead might save the day.

Who knew? Stranger things had happened...

I was ready for my juicy justice boner. So far it had all been foreplay. It was time to get down to business.

CHAPTER SEVEN

"DID YOU LEARN ANYTHING?" I ASKED CANDY WHILE WE KEPT
our heads down and made our way through the crowd over to
the area where Anne Boleyn had been murdered by King
Henry the Eighth. It had become evident that the Demons,
Angels and Nephilim in attendance were the dregs of
Immortal society. Most were armed to the teeth, and shady-
looking was a polite way to describe them.

"Not much, jackass," Candy Vargo replied. "How about you,
freaks?"

I lowered my voice to a whisper. "Well, I dusted three
Demons and Gideon offed another. The Immortals and
Nephilim are here to see the Angel of Mercy grant Immortality
to the Dragon King."

"Fuck, I turned the wrong way when we arrived," she
muttered. "What else?"

I pulled her off the path to a secluded area. Our posse
followed. "The dead here know of two new ghosts but don't
know where they are."

"How are you having all the fun?" she demanded.

I gave her a look. "I wouldn't call any of this fun."

She shrugged. "You say tomato, I say motherfuckin' taaa-maaatoe."

I wanted to shake her, but that would end poorly. Candy Vargo was Candy Vargo. She wasn't going to change.

We'd made it up the hill and had a decent view of a guillotine. If memory served, she was beheaded with a sword. But then again, I wasn't well versed in Tudor royal history.

"Tell me what you know about Anne Boleyn's death," I said.

"Welp," Candy said, leaning in. "First off, she was innocent. Died like a true badass on the Tower Green. That fucker Henry called in the sword executioner from France before the woman was even tried. She was convicted on trumped-up bullshit charges 'cause that randy bastard already had a new wife picked out—charges included adultery, incest, and conspiracy against the King. Asshole wanted sons but kept gettin' daughters. He'd get pissed and murder his wife to marry another. Stupid asshole… sperm decides the sex of a child."

"I thought it was a sword," I said, impressed that I'd gotten one fact correct.

Candy nodded. "Yep. I suppose you could say Henry was being *nice*. Normally, they had some axe wielding jackhole to behead people. Usually took three to four whacks before the head was removed. The dude from France was an expert. Used a sword and lopped poor Anne's head off in one blow. All happened so fast there wasn't no coffin to bury her in. She was put into a box and buried under the floor of the chapel back behind where she was decapitated. Really shitty form if you ask me."

My stomach cramped at the thought of all of that. What was wrong with people?

"Were you there?" Dimple asked Candy.

Candy Vargo looked up into the cloudless winter sky for a long moment. "Unfortunately, I was. Anne Boleyn was my friend. I may or may not have been instrumental in the jousting accident that fucked that fucker up good."

"I want to be Candy Vargo when I grow up," Lura Belle announced.

"Shut your damn mouth. I ain't nobody to look up to," Candy Vargo chastised the Nephilim. However, the smile she couldn't hide gave away her delight at Lura Belle's words.

Gabe scrubbed his hands over his face then groaned. "As much as I hate—and mean *hate*—to say this, growing up to be like Candy Vargo isn't such a bad thing. As long as you don't eat people, you'll be fine."

"For the love of everything fuckin' unnecessary," Candy griped. "When are we gonna let the past be the past?"

"Let me think," Gabe said, pretending to put on a thinking cap then wrinkling his brow in deep thought. "Never. We will never let that be in the past. If we do, it could repeat itself."

"Fuck you," Candy grumbled.

"The sentiment is returned," he replied.

"Guys," I said, trying not to laugh. Cannibalism wasn't a laughing matter, but in the end, that episode turned out fine. I didn't know how, and I never wanted to know how, but it did. "Focus on the now."

"Agreed. There's a guillotine up there," Gabe pointed out. "No French guy with a sword in sight."

All eyes went to the area called Tower Green.

"No one said Micky Muggles was well-read or smart," Gideon said. "Further proof he's not the reincarnated version of King Henry."

I glanced over at him. "Do you believe in that?"

He was quiet for a long beat. "Honestly, I don't know, Daisy.

Kind of a nice thought if it was truly granted to those whose lives had been taken for no good reason, but... I suppose I'll have to be satisfied with not knowing the answer to the question."

It was confusing to think about. In my not very religious brain, I'd come to the conclusion that once people went into the Light or the Darkness, they stayed there. The thought that Steve could come back was surreal. Of course, it wouldn't be him. It would be someone else entirely. I pushed the line of thinking away. Getting lost in what ifs was nuts. No juicy justice boner would be achieved if I wasn't fully present.

We stayed at the back of the crowd. When Micky Muggles walked out the cheers were loud mixed with equally loud boos. It didn't throw him at all. He just pumped his scrawny arms over his head and then took a bow. The redneck looked the same. With his mullet and beer belly he personified the sadistic loser he was. Most of his ass had grown back. He stood on the platform where the guillotine was set up and scanned the crowd. His gaze stopped on our group for half a beat too long then moved on.

"There's no way he recognizes us," I hiss-whispered to Candy Vargo.

"Not a chance," she replied. "However, he ain't as dumb as he looks. We'll just stay back. Playin' our hand now without knowin' where Gram, Tory and Mr. Jackson are ain't happening."

"Agreed." I looked at the three Nephilim and seriously doubted the wisdom of keeping them with us. We knew Micky Muggles was here. We knew Tory, Gram and Mr. Jackson were here. I'd never forgive myself if Jolly Sue, Lura Belle or Dimple died.

Gideon glanced over at me. It was as if the man could read

my mind. *"Do you want me to get them out? I don't think we need them and at this point they could be a liability."*

"Roger that," I replied. *"Take them back to Tim and let him know what's going on, please."*

"On it. They're going to be pissed."

"I'm sure they will be, but I'd much rather have them alive and pissed than dead and hanging out at our house for years to come... or permanently."

"Holy shit," he muttered with a pained chuckle. *"I'll be back shortly."*

"Where are we going?" Dimple asked, wildly confused as Gideon moved to usher them back down the hill.

"To Tim," I told her. "You'll be safer there."

Lura Belle's eyebrows shot up, and she pursed her lips. Even though she might look like a teenager, she was still the cat-butt lipped old lady deep down. "You're making a mistake, mewling maggot-pie."

"Not to worry," Jolly Sue told her sister, giving me the stink-eye. "We'll be back when you least expect it. Don't forget we have a knob to gnaw."

Lura Belle was astonished. "So you're willing to chomp the chubby?"

"I am," Jolly Sue announced.

They both turned to Dimple, crossed their arms over their chests and waited. "Fine," she snapped. "I shall polish off the pecker. But hear me now... this is the last time I will ingest genitals. Period."

We were starting to get funny looks from sketchy and armed passers-by. It was time to get the gals out of here.

Silently, and with some serious bad attitudes, they slipped away. I blew out an audible sigh of relief.

"Good thinkin', fucker," Candy said, patting me on the back.

"If those old bats kept goin' with the sixteenth century insults, Micky Muggles would have pegged us for sure."

A zing of dread whipped through me. I hadn't even considered that possibility. "They're gone and safe."

Gabe kept his eyes on the gathered crowd and scanned it constantly. I didn't think Tory would be in attendance, but with the Dragon King, who knew.

"Are we really going to watch someone get beheaded for no good reason other than Micky Muggles is an egomaniacal assbag?" I asked Candy.

She spit her toothpick out of her mouth and pulled a fresh one from her pocket. "Nope. If it comes to it, I'll chant a little spell that'll freeze the guillotine. Not to worry."

Again, I sighed in relief. I'd had some messed-up days, but this one took the cake for disconcerting.

Gabe didn't look at us when he spoke. His eyes were now glued to Micky's every move. "I say we follow the son-of-bitch after the failed beheading. It might lead us directly to where we want to be."

"I'll let the dead know to follow him too," I added.

As if on cue, Gragraunch—or whatever his actual name was —appeared beside me.

"Haaaavah suuuurpriiiizeah," he said, quivering with excitement.

"You found Gram and Mr. Jackson?" I asked the ghost.

"Yeeeesah!"

"Tory? The human Immortal? She has silver hair and was with Gram and Mr. Jackson."

"Nooooooah. Soorrrryah."

We were two thirds of the way there with being able to find Gram and Mr. Jackson. We were here for the juicy boner of justice. We'd find Tory too.

"Can you let the ghosts know where I am?"

"Yeeeesah!"

"Thank you," I told him, touching his face. His sunken eyes grew misty at my gesture. I had plans to take Gragraunch home with me. He deserved better. "Also, Gragraunch, can you and the other ghosts follow Micky Muggles, please? I need to know where he goes. It's imperative for the life of my friend, Tory."

"Asssssah yoooouah wisssshhhah," he replied then zipped away.

At this point my army consisted of several insanely powerful Immortals and a gaggle of ghosts. It was a little unusual but was par for the course for me.

"Good plan, asshole," Candy said.

Her terms of endearment didn't bother me anymore. I kind of liked them. Gideon walked back up after being gone only a few minutes. His casual gait and calm demeanor didn't set any alarm bells off in my head, but I couldn't understand how he'd gotten the gals back to Tim so quickly.

Unless... I quickly looked back at the platform. Micky Muggles was still there. Had he gotten so good at becoming other people that he could be in two freaking places at once? When he'd scanned the crowd, his gaze had stayed on us a bit too long. Was the Keeper of Fate incorrect? Had he recognized us?

"Don't speak to Gideon until after I do," I insisted to Gabe and Candy.

My brother's body went rigid, and Candy began to glow a little.

"Tamp that crap back," I snapped at her.

She obeyed.

"You think it's not him?" she asked under her breath.

"I'm not sure," I replied. "If it is, I'm not sure he actually took the gals back to Tim. The timing is way the heck off. He's meticulous. This doesn't jive."

Gabe's tone was scary. "If that's not Gideon. He dies."

"Obviously," I hissed quietly.

The Grim Reaper approached us while keeping his eye on our surroundings. He was still short, dumpy and sporting a receding hairline, but I was almost a hundred percent sure he was himself. Although, I thought Heather was herself when she wasn't.

"Hey babe, that was quick," I said, forcing a smile and hoping my voice wasn't as tight as my stomach felt.

He stopped and tilted his head. "Yes, it was."

"Did it… umm… go alright?"

He gave me an odd look. I kept talking. If he wasn't Gideon, we were screwed. It meant that Micky Muggles had way more power than we believed.

"Where have you been?" I asked. If Gideon was actually *Gideon,* he was going to think I'd lost it.

The Grim Reaper caught on quickly. "Ask me."

"Umm… I just did," I replied, backing away as Gabe and Candy flanked me.

"The safe word. Ask me the safe word." He was calm, cool and completely collected.

Getting my shit together was top priority. I felt like an idiot. "Safe word, please."

Gideon leaned in. "Juicy justice boner. And you were smart to ask. I took the Nephilim back to the alcove and transported them to Tim. After a very brief update, I transported back."

My knees felt like they might buckle. Gabe held me up. "I'm sorry."

"Nope," the love of my life said firmly. "You did the right thing. No chances need to be taken."

Gabe touched my arm to get my attention. Micky Muggles was about to speak.

"I feel Tory," he whispered, glancing around wildly. "She's near. I swear on the Light, if he tries to behead her, every single person here will die. Violently."

"Dude," Candy said, slapping the back of his head. "One, you're glowing. Cut that shit out. Two, if you try to kill me history *will* repeat itself, and I will eat you. We clear on that, fucker?"

"He didn't mean us," I said, pretty sure I was right. I glanced over at my brother. His laser focus was on Micky Muggles.

"Welcome to my castle," Micky yelled to the gathered crowd. "I am the DRAGON KING."

"Yeah, yeah," a snarly Demon heckled. "But you're not Immortal, are ya? You're just a weak, pathetic Nephilim with an embarrassing haircut."

The dangerous and despicable audience roared with laughter. Although the Nephilim in the crowd were pissed to be insulted, they laughed as well. If the half-Angel, half-humans went at the Immortals this would turn into a bloodbath.

"He's a blowhard," another Demon shouted. "This is bullshit."

Micky Muggles' beady eyes narrowed to slits. He might not be Immortal, but he wasn't without magic. I wasn't sure if the Demons knew what a powerful, delusional fool they were dealing with. Not that they were anything to write home about...

"SILENCE," the self-proclaimed Dragon King roared. "Lemme tell you somethin', you low-life shitasses. I've been alive for a thousand fuckin' years! Show me another weak

95

pathetic Nephilim that's done that." Spittle flew from his thin lips and his mannerisms became jerky. "I'm the DRAGON KING. I've banged more big-busted beauties than all of you put together."

"Were they blow-up dolls?" another yelled. "Or blind?"

Micky was about to lose it. "I will not take that backtalk," he screamed. His face was blood red and his feather-bare wings popped out of his back. They were mangy and molting, but it impressed his low-brow audience. "I will become Immortal shortly."

He raised his spark-shooting hands above his head. The Nephilim cheered on one of their own. The Demons and Angels grew warier by the second.

"Be ready to take cover," I instructed my crew then leaned into Gideon. "Did Tim have any clue how time ran in here?"

He shook his head. "No, but from the Dragon King's deranged claim, it's running differently. Or, he's just lost his mind along with control over his army of scum."

"I'm goin' for box number two!" a very familiar voice whispered in my ear. "My boyfriend, Bob Barker, always liked box number two better, Daisy girl."

My joy at hearing her voice ripped through me and a squeak that sounded like I'd swallowed helium left my lips.

Gideon, Gabe and Candy Vargo—who had tears of relief in her eyes at seeing Gram—surrounded us to shield us from any prying eyes. The Keeper of Fate wiggled her fingers and sound proofed the area around us. I got low and gently pulled Gram down with me. My eyes frantically searched her from head to toe to make sure she was in one piece. She was fine. When Mr. Jackson popped up beside her from out of thin air, I held back my startled yelp with effort.

"How did you find me?" I asked, checking Mr. Jackson over.

He was not looking great, but his macabre smile spoke volumes about his lovely character. If it was Gargraunch, he'd worked fast.

"Graaaaagrainchah," Mr. Jackson shared. "Goooodah maaannnn."

"That's right," Gram agreed, patting Mr. Jackson on the back. "Oh, sweetie pie, these ghosts here just break my heart to bits. But I tell you what, it gets my dang knickers in a knot that they didn't know there was help available. Some of these poor souls have been hangin' around since the Lord created underpants. I've been runnin' round Hell's half acre trying to let them know your address, darlin'."

I gulped but didn't comment.

"Has to be about three hundred fallin' apart dead fellas and gals here," she said, shaking her head in sorrow. "I've been busier than a one-legged cat in a litter box."

"Tory," I said urgently. "Is she okay?"

Gram's expression hardened. "Weak but okay for now. That egg-sucking, mullet-wearin' dawg has been sippin' on her blood. Keepin' my Tory from gettin' back to business."

Gabe growled low in his throat. The sound was chilling. He turned to face Gram. His voice was the definition of pain and raw fury. "Where is she?"

"Tooooowahhh," Mr. Jackson said. "Talllah tooooowahhh."

"Will you take me there?" he asked the kind dead man.

"Yeeeesah!"

I made the calls fast and from my gut. Gabe was too emotionally invested to be rational. Tory needed someone with a cool head and a hell of a lot of magic. I wasn't sure if Micky Muggles was about to behead someone, but if so, Candy could help me stop it. The decision was made.

"Gideon, go with Gabe. I'll stay here with Candy."

"Agreed," he said. "If... No. When we find her, Gabe will transport her out, and I'll return to you. I'd like a front row seat for the demise of the dragon."

"Might need your help with that one," I told him.

"The pleasure will be all mine, fiancée," he replied as he ran his thumb over my lips then turned to follow Gabe and Mr. Jackson.

"Well, butter my butt and call me a biscuit," Gram gushed, admiring my ring. "It's about time! I'm just tickled pink."

"About that," Candy Vargo said. "You gonna get hitched soon? I need to brush up on my skills before I perform the fuckin' ceremony."

I wrinkled my nose. "Are you going to use the word fuck in the vows?"

She pondered that for a bit while she kept an eye on the crowd. "Yep. Yep, I am."

I wasn't surprised. It wouldn't be a celebration without Candy dropping an F-bomb or three.

"Lemme tell you something, Candy Vargo," Gram said, getting in her face. "I love ya like I birthed ya, but I'm gonna wash your dang mouth out with soap for a month. You will not be droppin' no F-bombs at Daisy's weddin'. You hear me?"

"Yes, ma'am," Candy said contritely. The Keeper of Fate might be one of the Universe's biggest badasses, but Gram had her wrapped around her dead pinkie finger.

"Candy, the answer to your question is, I don't know. We just got engaged. Talk to me again after we get out of here alive," I said.

"Houston, we have a problem," Candy growled. "Gram, I want to you to skedaddle. Now."

"Will do, darlin'. You girls be safe," she said as she zipped away.

My name was Daisy, but I caught Candy's movie reference. She was correct. The Dragon King's people seemed to be turning on him. It was about to get messy.

"That idiot's been goin' on about his prowess in bed and his dick size. I'm pretty sure he lost his audience."

"Wait. What?" I asked, as I tuned back into the evil bastard's monologue.

"You will obey the Dragon King," Micky Muggles bellowed. He paced the guillotine platform erratically. His sorry excuse for wings flapped in the wind and began to fall off. However, his hands were on fire. I'd experienced his fire-balls. They were deadly. "I am the Supreme Leader. Once the Angel of Mercy gives me my Immortality, you will destroy her."

"Fucker's on drugs," Candy said with a grunt of disgust.

"Next on the hit list is the Keeper of Fate, the Archangel Gabriel and the Grim Reaper," Micky Muggles commanded.

Candy bit her toothpick in half and chewed it like it was gum.

"Are you fucking insane?" an enormous Demon with his horns protruding out of his head shouted.

"I want no part of that, you imbecile," another yelled. "It would destroy the balance and the world would end."

"NO," Micky shrieked and blasted the Demon who spoke with a fireball that turned him to ash. His display of lethal magic silenced the crowd immediately. His rant continued. "It will not end because I say it won't. And I can prove it. I have the Immortal Purgatory, and I will behead her to prove my point."

I grabbed Candy's hand at his announcement about Tory and squeezed it hard.

High on his own Kool-aid, Micky exclaimed, "She's my

fuckin' Anne Boleyn! Y'all will obey me because I am your KING."

"Will that shit for brains really try to kill his bargainin' chip?" Candy Vargo asked, trying to get a feel for what he might truly do.

"Maybe he'll piss people off so bad, we won't have to kill him because they will," I said softly.

She shook her head. "Nope, I feel a change in the wind."

"Shit," I muttered, praying hard that Gideon and Gabe had found Tory and gotten her out of harm's way. The fact that Gideon hadn't returned yet wasn't a good sign, but I could still hope.

One of the Demons crawled up onto the platform with Micky. He glared at the gathered group then spat on the ground. "The asshole is crazy, but he might be onto something."

"What?" a female Angel snarled. "The Apocalypse?"

"Fuck that," the Demon on the stage roared. "We've been held down by lies for eternity. How do we know the balance wasn't something dreamed up by the Gods and Goddesses to hold us back. It's all bullshit. We will rule our own destiny. Kill the Angel of Mercy. Kill the Keeper of Fate. Kill the Archangel Gabriel. Kill the Grim Reaper. KILL THEM ALL."

"What he said," Micky Muggles screeched, looking more unhinged by the second. "What's your name, Demon?"

"I go by Killer."

The man with the mullet pointed at the man with the horns. "Killer's gonna be my second in command. If you follow me, we're gonna own the world. Them humans will be fair game. We will take what we deserve and kill anyone who don't want us to have it. Every Immortal who don't obey me will rue the day they was born. Because I am the DRAGON KING."

Micky Muggles danced like he was wasted on the platform. As he spastically gyrated, he removed his clothing. It was revolting.

His people followed suit.

Candy and I did not. The Keeper of Fate yanked me behind a small stone wellhouse. We got low and watched the weirdest display of I-don't-even-know-what go down.

"Welp," Candy said, rolling her eyes. "If they're all nekkid, they won't have no weapons on 'em. Makes 'em easier to dust."

Leave it to Candy Vargo to find a bright side. "I guess there's that."

The new leader of the naked freaks grabbed his penis and swung it like a lasso—albeit a tiny one. "The Dragon King's power is in the tail. All hail the tail."

Over a hundred naked Immortals and Nephilim bowed to the Dragon King's pathetic package. If I wasn't living this moment, I wouldn't have believed it.

And then something seriously bad happened. A beaten and battered Tory was dragged to the platform by her hair. Gabe and Gideon had not found her in the tower. She wasn't safe. She was about to lose her head.

The nude army of degenerates screamed their approval. My beautiful and powerful friend had almost been drained dry of her blood. She was normally pale, but she looked ashen and broken. She was held by two of Micky's new henchmen, and her slim neck was placed on the base of the guillotine.

"Son of a motherfucker," Candy Vargo hissed as she waved her hand and removed our disguises.

"Ghosts," I shouted. I didn't care who heard me. The time to hide was over. "Come to me."

It was time to stop the madness.

CHAPTER EIGHT

We weren't far from the action—about a quarter of a football field away. The Dragon King and his people were so focused on the decapitation about to go down, that no one noticed the gathering of ghosts who had heeded my call. Gram had greatly underestimated the number of dead in the Tower of London. Just as Candy Vargo had underestimated the number of Demons, Angels and Nephilim inside the walls. At least three hundred dead hovered around me. They were in all sorts of states of decomposition. While I'd seen specters in bad shape, I'd never witnessed anything like this.

Gragraunch and Gram were the de facto leaders of the transparent army.

I didn't waste any time. "Tory can touch the dead like I can. You're corporal to her," I told them. Ghosts normally went right through people. As the Death Counselor, I could touch them—not always but most of the time. Tory could touch them as well. I had no idea why, but I wasn't about to look a gift horse in the mouth. Instead, I hoped I could use it to my advantage… and Tory's. "The latch on the guillotine isn't secure. On masse, I believe you can push her out of the guillo-tine and move her to safety."

"You bet your bippy we can," Gram grunted. "We ain't gonna let that piece of junk with the heart of a thumpin' gizzard do our gal no more harm. Tory's head is far too pretty to be lopped off by a loser. Dead people, we're gonna make some noise! And when I say noise, I mean yip like your life depends on it."

"Weeeeeeeeeee areeeah deaaaadah," Gragraunch reminded her.

"My bad!" Gram slapped herself in the head. "These days, I don't know whether to check my bee-hind or scratch my watch! Hoot and holler like your *afterlife* depends on it," she amended.

Gram got a garbled and unintelligible response, but from the enthusiastic nodding and loss of a few precariously attached heads, it appeared they understood.

"Go, go GO!" I commanded as Candy Vargo handed me a toothpick.

"We're goin' for the dead fucker walkin'," she said. "We're gonna get pushback from the nekkid bastards in the peanut gallery, but once the tail—or rather pecker—has been removed, we'll take care of the rest of 'em."

"Sounds like a plan. Kind of a bad one."

"You got somethin' better?" she demanded, glowing like a firework on the Fourth of July. She was terrifying, and I was seriously happy she was on my team.

"I do. I go for the mullet asshole, and you cover me. Hope-fully, Gideon and Gabe will show up and we'll get our juicy justice boner. However, even without them, we're gonna cut that tail off that donkey."

"Badass," Candy said with a grin. "Let's go slay the dragon."

"Let's."

It was shockingly beautiful to watch three hundred ghosts fly together with a single purpose. They flew like they'd been pent up for centuries and had just discovered light. The whoosh of that many transparent bodies soaring through the air sounded like a howling wind that foretold death and destruction. Individually, they looked like people. Together, they reminded me of a snow squall—a flurry of righteous purpose blasting from the clouds above. Their flight was for justice—the juicy kind.

Micky Muggles' army of douchebags didn't know what to make of it. The Nephilim took off running like the Darkness was on their heels. That cut his followers in half. We were now facing about a hundred and fifty, give or take, Immortals. The Demons transformed from human-looking beings into eight-foot-tall stinking hulks of sulfur with blue and green flames dancing over their skin. The Angels—who were far fewer in numbers than the Demons—morphed as well. Their wings burst from their backs as they huddled together in confusion.

While most of the dead kept Micky's throng occupied, a small group of the ghosts swooped to the stage without notice. My eyes widened when they grabbed Tory by the feet and yanked her out of the guillotine and between her distracted Demon guards.

I gave a shout of victory as I watched a dozen more specters form a wall between the Demons and Tory. It wouldn't stop the Immortals, but it made them pause for the few seconds Tory's rescuers needed to float her away to safety. It was a glorious sight.

The Dragon King didn't seem concerned that his bargaining chip was getting away.

"I know you're here, Angel of Mercy," he screamed, jerking

his head left and right in a tizzy. "Show yourself, Daisy. We have some business to finish, bitch."

"Sounds like our cue," Candy Vargo said with a grin. "Transport or walk?"

"Walk," I replied.

Only two steps in, I felt Gideon's presence by my side.

"What's a beautiful girl like you doing in a shithole like this?" he inquired as if we weren't walking into a bunch of clothing-impaired and insane Immortals who wanted us dead.

I shrugged and smiled. "I dunno," I shot back. "Thought I'd get a little castration out of my system today."

"Sounds like a plan."

"And just so you know, the Dragon Derp has given orders to his army to kill you, Candy, Gabe and me."

"Interesting," Gideon said. "And is there a reason they're naked?"

"Your guess is as good as mine." I glanced around but didn't see my brother. "Where's Gabe?"

"We came back as the ghosts were extracting Tory from the guillotine. He's with her."

"Perfect." The news made my heart happy. Tory was vulnerable right now and Gabe was the exact right person to protect her. I was glad his focus was on the woman he loved instead of revenge.

Candy waved her hand. The Grim Reaper was no longer short, sporting a gut and working a receding hairline. Nope. He was back to his usual self—stunningly hot.

"There she is," Micky squawked, pointing at me. "It's the Angel of Mercy. You got my immortality with you?"

"Actually, no. That's not happening." My words were matter-of-fact. My tone could have frozen water.

We'd walked right into the center of the area where the

enemy had gathered. My impossibly powerful trio formed a back-to-back triangle in the middle of the chaos. The herd of half-wits, loyal to an imbecile, backed away from us. Of course, my dangerously sparking hands, Gideon's red fire-spitting eyes and the undeniable fact that Candy Vargo looked like she might detonate at any moment probably helped.

"I thought you'd say that," Micky replied smugly while playing with his flaccid penis. I didn't know whether to laugh or puke. I did neither. I kept my gaze on his ugly face. "But ya know, there's more than one way to skin a chicken."

"You pluck a chicken," I said.

"What?" he shouted, confused.

"A chicken has feathers," I said with an eye roll. "You don't skin it. You pluck it."

"There's a tree stump in Alabama smarter than him," Gram yelled from the mass of ghosts floating above the fray.

The laughter from the naked yet still very dangerous horde infuriated the self-proclaimed King. In a fit of rage, Micky Muggles threw a massive fireball, incinerating a third of his army. Two things came from that. One, they seemed to be turning against their leader. Two, they also seemed to be turning against each other. Both scenarios worked for me. The insanity level rose. Shouts of rage and infighting started. I wasn't sure who they hated more Micky Muggles, each other, or us.

"Kill the Grim Reaper and the Keeper of Fate," Micky roared above the noise and confusion. "Keep the Angel of Mercy ALIVE. I'm gonna kill her dead so hard she ain't gonna know what hit her. In about ten minutes, I'm gonna be the Angel of Mercy."

"What the fuck are you talking about?" his second in command, Killer, snarled.

Micky Muggles laughed like a maniac. Drool dripped down his chin, and snot flew from his nose. "Didn't y'all know? Whoever kills the Angel of Mercy becomes the next Angel of Mercy. AND IT'S GONNA BE ME."

I got my answer as to who the army was loyal to. It wasn't the Dragon King, and it definitely wasn't us. They'd just been given the key to the Kingdom, and killing me to take my job was now the goal. I hadn't wanted the job as the Angel of Mercy. However, no naked low-life was going to take it from me.

"Motherfucker," Candy Vargo growled as everyone came at us from all sides at once.

I'd had a bounty on my head for a while now, but this was not good.

Slashing my arms through the air, I popped a few crazed Demons who were gunning for me. The sound was gross. The result was not. If it was them or me, I preferred it be them. Gideon was on fire from head to toe and taking down the enemy with ease. The problem was that there were a whole lot of them.

The ghosts flew in and out of the battle, trying to obscure the view of our aggressors. That wasn't working. Transparent body parts were flying willy-nilly. Candy Vargo was a sight to behold, chopping off heads and dismembering people like it was a psychopathic game of Whack-a-Mole. She cackled like a loon as she got a two-for-one—two heads, one sword swipe.

I was bleeding from a head wound and beginning to lose hope. Not only was I fighting off cretins, I was also dodging Micky Muggles fireballs. I'd been hit by one once. I didn't want a repeat.

"Fucker's too strong," Candy shouted as she ripped the leg off of a Demon and beat him to a pulp with it.

"He's been drinking Tory's blood," I hollered back as I ducked another fireball while removing the head of a Demon who didn't want to take no for an answer. I was covered in my blood and his. If I lived, I was going to have to take a two-hour shower to wash all the violence away.

"Hey fuckers," Candy bellowed. She was bleeding profusely and grinning like a fool. "Wally said something smart. *When you have exhausted all possibilities, remember this: you haven't.*"

He had said that... or Thomas A. Edison had. Honestly, it didn't matter who said it. It was profound and gave me the boost of energy I needed to keep fighting. I just hoped and prayed that I had enough in me to go after my goal—ending Micky Muggles reign of terror for good. At the rate this was going, I wasn't sure.

"Freedom from bullshit," Killer growled as he went for Candy. "You're gonna DIE!"

She laughed and grabbed the Demon in a chokehold that wasn't going to end well for him.

"Only three places you can stay for free and bullshit ain't one of them," the Keeper of Fate snarled in his ear. "The places you can stay for free are, in your own fuckin' lane, over there or out the fuck of my business."

There was no time for Killer to respond. His head was gone from his body right as Candy spoke the last word.

Gideon took a hit from a duo of Demons before returning it tenfold. They literally blew up. Gut and innards spattered everywhere, and I gagged. "There's too many," he said, incinerating an Angel who tried unsuccessfully to remove his head.

"No shit," I grunted, then drop-kicked an Angel and tore off his wings. His shrieks were piercing. I didn't care.

"Are they multiplying?" Gideon shouted as he fought off more.

"Feels like it," I said, dodging another fireball headed my way, compliments of the Dragon King.

"We could use a little fuckin' backup," Candy bellowed, as a sword chopped into her shoulder, the appendage barely hanging on by a tendon. "This is chappin' my ass."

My fingers sparked, and I could feel a destructive magic bubbling inside me. It was dark. I was going with it. Slashing both hands through the air, I envisioned blades of fire. The appeared in my hands immediately. With a guttural scream of rage and exhaustion, I threw them at the evil dudes headed for me. My blades hit their targets with a sizzle followed by horrified shrieks.

"That was a four in one, motherfucker!" Candy crowed with pride at my killing ability.

I'd rather be known for my sense of humor and my kindness, but that time was long gone. The world I inhabited was violent and deadly, and every time I thought we had the advantage, more Demons and Angels arrived. I was strong, but even the strong needed a break. I was freaking exhausted.

Just when I thought all hope was lost, an unfathomable miracle happened. I didn't know if it was dumb luck or divine intervention. Maybe the Keeper of Fate had willed it or seen it coming. Either way, I didn't care. I'd never witnessed a more beautifully terrifying vision in my life.

"Hold on," Candy shouted in glorious triumph. "It's not over until the drag queens lip sync for our lives."

Atop their steeds, the Four Horsemen of the Apocalypse galloped onto the warring field of Immortals. They were in full-on terrifying Armageddon-is-coming-for-you regalia, complete with scary fucking horns, sharp, nightmare-inducing fangs and hollowed-out skeletal faces. And, of course, they had on hand-beaded gowns. It was a juxtaposition of horror and high fashion.

Dirk, also known as Death, rode on a pale green steed. He'd been created as a tool of destruction and looked every bit the part. The glistening, emerald-beaded frock only made the picture scarier. His eyes were glittering black and looked soulless.

Fred was next to him. He was known as Famine. He, too, had been created as a tool of destruction. All four of them were. His massive steed was as black as Fred's eyes and he was here for business. If I wasn't mistaken, and I wasn't, he was wearing a diamond tiara around one of his gnarled horns.

Carl rode alongside Fred. His fangs were glowing equally as bright as his razor-sharp horns. He was known as Conquest. His horse was white, and his growl of fury shook the foundation of the Tower of London. The marabou trim on his gown only added to his deadly charm.

Wally rounded up the gang of some of my favorite people in the Universe. He was as adept at talking about high heels as he was discussing ripping a head off and kicking it through a goalpost. He was known as War. It was apt. The gleaming sword he held in his free hand had to be five feet long. His horse was red, and his emotionless eyes matched his comrades'—glittering black. Wally, always one to match his eyes to his outfit, wore his ebony-beaded gown with pride.

What I didn't expect was that they'd have passengers. Candy's disguise spells had obviously been broken. I recognized the others by what they normally looked like—not by their essence.

Tim rode with Dirk.

Jolly Sue rode with Fred.

Lura Belle rode with Carl.

And Dimple was with Wally.

Tim was back in his mail uniform and looked every bit the Immortal badass Courier he was. He might be a mild-mannered sweetheart who couldn't cook to save his life on the daily, but as the Immortal Courier, he was a force to be reckoned with. His eyes glowed eerily, and his expression was one of barely restrained ire.

Dimple, Jolly Sue and Lura Belle were dressed in their go-to conservative Chanel pantsuits. The sensible shoes were back, and they gnashed their teeth in anticipation of biting off the Dragon's tail. Or castration by chompers, to be more accurate.

I was concerned for their safety, but they were not. They slid off the massive horses and calmly walked over to me.

The stunned silent army of scumbags was petrified. Literally. None of them batted an eyelash or moved a hair. It wasn't every day that one was in the presence of those who were foretold to end the world, and the Demons and Angels weren't trying to attract any apocalyptic energy their way.

The Grim Reaper was never one to miss an advantageous opening and took it. He roared then began chanting in a language I'd never heard. Sparks of fire detonated with each word. He got down on his knees and slammed the ground with his fists, causing four-foot craters to appear beneath the feet of all who had tried to end us. In a flash of blood-red lightning, they were sucked into the holes.

Gideon stood up, clapped his hands, and closed the craters. Casually, he brushed the dirt off his jeans. There was still blood caked all over them, but his coolness factor was high.

The ghosts went nuts. The applauding dead created a wind that came close to blowing me off my feet. I almost smiled. Almost.

"Where the hell did you send those bastards?" Candy questioned.

Gideon's mouth thinned into a grim smile that didn't meet his eyes. It was hot, sexy and scary. "To the Darkness. The punishments there will far outweigh anything we could do here."

"Excellent," Dirk said, eyeing the lone bad guy with disgust.

We weren't done yet.

The Dragon King was still in our midst, and he hadn't given up.

"Well, now that was kinda show-offy," the deluded jerk purred. He rubbed his hands together and grinned like an idiot. "I betcha you think you're just gonna off my ass and go on home to your nice little life. Doncha, Daisy?"

I watched him with narrowed eyes. He was still on the platform. He was still dangerous. Behind him and to the left, mostly obscured by a tree, stood Tory and Gabe. Gabe raised his finger to his lips and motioned us to look away. He was calm and focused. Tory still looked bad, but not as terrible as she'd looked only an hour ago. The Archangel had clearly been healing her with magic. She was not at full strength, but she wasn't the walking dead.

"Answer me, bitch," Micky Muggles roared as he continued to rub his hands together even faster.

"What's the fucker doin'?" Candy muttered softly.

"Not a clue," I heard Tim answer.

"Well, Micky," I said with a shrug. "That was the plan. Do you have a problem with that?" The chance of him killing me when I was surrounded by the Immortals present was slim, but he was stupid-clever, and he'd proven repeatedly that his cleverness could spell disaster for us.

"Actually, I do have a problem with that," he replied and raised his arms over his head.

In his dirty, small hands sat a ball of silver-blue magic. It was mesmerizing.

"This is bad," Gideon ground out. "He's absorbed a lot of Tory's magic through her blood. We might be fucked."

I didn't get that. When Micky had abducted Gideon, Gabe, Zander and Zander's sister Catriona, he'd partaken in their blood. The was a shitload of magic. How was Tory's blood different?

"Not following," I said. "How is he more powerful on Tory's blood than yours?"

"Purgatory's power eclipses all others," Gideon explained. "It gives her the ability to control the Souls of the Martyrs."

"Not what I wanted to hear," I muttered as I wondered how much longer we could go on. The sage advice of the Four Horseman began to dance in my weakening mind. Fred had advised, *Strength does not come from physical capacity. It comes from indomitable will.* Physical strength I had... but was my will strong enough?

The blue magic above Micky's head was almost white now as sliver tendrils wove in and out of the giant ball of light—like diamonds dancing on the sun. I'd never seen anything like it before. Micky Muggles began to grunt and gyrate. With each repulsive move, he made the ball grow bigger... and bigger.

"Fuck," Gideon snarled through gritted teeth. "We kill him now, or we all die."

Micky Muggles continued to undulate as the orb of powerful Purgatory magic continued to grow.

"How do we stop it?" I asked, trying to shove the Nephilim behind me. They were having none of it.

Wally pulled Candy Vargo and Tim onto his horse. "We

can't," he declared. "It's the strongest there is. All we can do is get out of its way."

"Shit," I grumbled. "Ghosts. LEAVE." I literally picked up Jolly Sue and tossed her to Dirk. Followed by the tossing of Lura Belle to Fred and Dimple to Carl. "Get them out of here. I'll handle it."

"We will handle it," Gideon corrected me.

"Like hell, you will," the Keeper of Fate grunted, trying to pull me and Gideon up onto the horse. "You can't survive it. Fucker drank most of Tory's blood. Fucker has Tory's magic. Ain't no one gonna live through gettin' blasted by that. Not even the baddest of asses."

Micky's deranged laughter filled the air as the sky darkened. A storm brewed and created its own eerie song in the leafless winter trees.

"If I can get to the tail, I can end this," I roared, running toward the sick man who wanted to be the Immortal King. "I want my juicy justice boner. And if I go down, I'm taking him with me."

Words and images raced through my mind as I sprinted toward the tail that would end the madness. Silently, I apologized to my daughter. If I died stopping the Dragon King so that she could live a full life, that would have to be my final gift to her. Maybe I could come back as a ghost. As her face faded in my mind, the words of the queens sprang forward.

I spoke them aloud to give me hope. "There are dark shadows on the earth, but its lights are stronger in contrast." I was the light. Micky Muggles was the dark shadow. I would prove I was stronger. I had to. "You must remember," I recited, "that out of our greatest battles come miracles."

I was all about miracles right now.

"Time to die, Daisy," Micky jeered, as he reared back with

the enormous ball in his slimy clutches. "There's gonna be a new Angel of Mercy in town. And I ain't got a drop of mercy in me."

And that was the moment my world went into slow motion and fell apart.

CHAPTER NINE

"Come on, Daisy," Micky Muggles bellowed. "Last time I blasted ya, ya lived. This time, ya ain't gonna be as lucky."

I zig-zagged across the field, dodging magical artillery flying from the silvery orb floating above his hands as I made my way closer to Micky. I could feel Gideon doing the same thing to my right, but I couldn't spare a glance in his direction. If I looked away from Micky, it might be the very last thing I'd ever do. At this point, the Grim Reaper might as well have gone home. The Dragon's focus was only on me.

Micky's face with beet red and contorted with rage as he missed me over and over.

Good. I was pissing him off.

Every time he aimed, he had to readjust. Tory's magic was powerful but heavy, and he strained to wield it. His arms shook from the weight. It was clear that creating the magic ball had drained him. If I could wear him out, he might drop the ball and destroy himself. I wasn't sure how big the blast would be or how precisely it needed to be thrown, but there was a chance that the Dragon might slay himself.

Trying to make it look like a running maneuver, I motioned to Gabe and Tory to leave the Tower. My brother shook his head, pointed to Micky Muggles and silently urged me to pay attention to staying alive. Tory's pale eyes were huge with worry, but she made it clear with a gesture that she was going nowhere fast. I didn't know what they had planned, but Tory understood her magic better than anyone here. Of course, since she wasn't wielding it, there was a chance she was as lost as I was.

"You can't win this," I yelled at Micky. "Even if you kill me, you'll be hunted like an animal until you're destroyed."

"Ya know, Daisy... you're gettin' on my last nerve," he snapped. "You've fucked around one too many times, and you're about to find out."

I'd keep him talking and distracted. "The grass is always greener on the other side because it's fertilized with bullshit, Micky."

"What in tarnation is that supposed to mean?" he growled, doing his best to line up a clear shot.

I wasn't going to make it easy for him. The fact that he hadn't thrown the Angel-of-Mercy-killing ball told me he probably could only make the one, and he was waiting for his moment to use it against me.

Unlike Micky's magic arsenal, an idea struck me. Maybe standing still for a moment would make him go for it. I'd just have to be ready to dodge it. He was weakened by using up the magic he'd stolen, and I couldn't see him throwing faster than I could run. I'd just have to bide my time.

It was time for a game. Micky Muggles hated word games. He'd flunked English in high school multiple times. I sent a silent thanks to Jennifer for teaching us the game on the car ride up.

"Shipments go by land, but cargo goes by sea. That needs to be reversed," I called out as I continued to weave closer.

"Quit that educated bullshit jabberin'," he snapped. "I ain't got no time for that."

"Almond milk should be called nut juice."

"SHUT UP," he screamed.

"A loaf of bread should be called raw toast," I said, flipping the mullet-wearing redneck the middle finger. Pissed-off people were messy. They made mistakes. Micky Muggles was one colossal mistake, but throwing him off his game could work to my advantage. "Tongs should be renamed salad tweezers."

"I said shut your mouth, bitch," he snarled. "You think you're so fancy livin' in a big house and havin' all them people kissin' your ass. I'm guessin' pretty soon all your fancy friends are gonna be kissin' MY ASS."

I laughed. "Your ass got bitten off if I'm remembering correctly."

"Fuck you," he shouted. "It grew back." He was getting erratic. His face was a mottled purple, his chest was heaving, and his magic tank was close to empty. The time to stand still for a moment so he could hurl the ball at me was coming soon. But not quite yet. The weaker he was, the shittier his aim, and the easier it would be to survive. "A better name for donuts is sugar bagels."

"I'm gonna kill you."

"Good luck with that," I shot back as I snaked a winding path through the grassy area. "Seagulls should be called beach chickens, and gloves should be called finger-pants."

If looks could kill, I'd be six feet under. They couldn't. I was getting closer to my tiny, flapping-in-the-wind target. I considered calling forth fire daggers again as my weapon of choice, but I couldn't chance that the deluded freak would see the blow coming. No. I needed a real blade. Once the asshole threw the ball, I would tuck and roll to his position and chop his foul tail clean from his body. The only thing standing between me and his demise with a massive, murderous ball of magical hate aimed in my direction.

Maybe Micky Muggles wasn't the only deluded fool on the green. Whatever. I didn't have a lot of options right now.

"Gideon," I said, keeping my eyes on Micky. "Do you still have the dagger in your sock?"

"I do," he replied. "Tell me what you're thinking."

"I'm wearing him down and pissing him off," I explained. "Seems to me he's almost drained of magic."

"I agree. Keep talking."

"Right," I said, weaving closer to the Grim Reaper. "Shortly, I'm going to stand still. When he throws, I dodge. Once the ball explodes, I'm going in and removing the tail. I'd rather avoid using my teeth. You feel me?"

"Jesus Christ," he said with a pained laugh. "I'd rather you didn't use your teeth as well. That would be a difficult visual to unsee."

"True that," I agreed. "Not sure an eternity of therapy could wipe that out. So... can I have the dagger?"

"Of course, but answer a question for me. Truthfully, Counselor."

"Ask, Reaper," I told him.

"How worn down are you from the battle? Do you know for certain that you can dodge the fireball?"

It was a fair question. I was ninety-nine-point-nine percent certain I could do it. Mind diving into the dead had resulted in some extra gifts—bizarre gifts. It had changed my DNA. I no longer wore glasses when I used to be almost blind without them, and I could run faster than an Alfa Romeo racing for a world championship. It was unclear if mind diving had resulted in my becoming Immortal or if it was when I had become the Angel of Mercy. Maybe it was a combination. It didn't matter. It just was.

Gideon asked for the truth. Even if he didn't like it, he would never try to stop me from doing my job, nor would I ever stop him from doing his. We loved and respected each other for who we were. *"Ninety-nine-point-nine percent sure,"* I told him. *"Which is incredibly good odds. However, I'll get him a little more off kilter before I stand still."*

"You've got this," he said. *"And I've got your back, fiancée."*

"I know you do, fiancé," I replied, smiling even though I wasn't looking at him. *"Candy Vargo is going to drop a few F-bombs during our vows."*

"That's unsurprising. I'm coming up behind you. Put your hand behind your back."

I did as he instructed. The dagger was in my hand two seconds later, and Micky Muggles was none the wiser. The cold steel felt cool against my skin. I tucked the blade into the back of my pants and kept moving.

"Thank you."

"Welcome," he responded. *"And remember... the icy blue magic will kill you. That's not up for debate. It's a fact. This is not a game. From the lore surrounding it, it will suck you into a vortex never to be seen or heard from again."*

The news made my stomach churn. However, there was no turning back. Micky Muggles had to be stopped. For good.

It was time for the last chapter of his story.

"Hey Micky," I called out as his eyes stayed glued to me and my haphazard movement. "You know something? You're not pretty enough to be as stupid as you are."

"As the NEW Angel of Mercy, I'm gonna send your mouthy ass to the Darkness," he screeched.

"Sounds like a plan," I told him with a smile that made him bare his teeth in fury. "But honestly, if I wanted to die, I'd climb your ego and jump from your IQ."

He was confused. My words were above his comprehension level.

He'd understand this one. It was at the level appropriate for a second-grade boy. "You look like a visible fart."

He got it, and he didn't like it. He was shaking with both the weight of the magic and rage. The time was now.

I pretended to trip. I'd have a better chance of avoiding death if I had a sprinter's start. The imbecile's laugh was maniacal. He thought he'd won.

Time slowed, or it felt as if it did.

The Dragon King screamed with joy. I pulled my feet back under me and stayed low in a squat... ready to take off to the right. I was so close. The enemy was naked, and the tail was in sight. Everything was going as planned.

Slowly, Micky raised his hands higher and reared back. His eyes were wild, and gibberish, along with strings of saliva, flew from his lips. The beachball-sized silvery magic in his hands shimmered in the late afternoon sun. Its beauty belied the devastating damage it could do, but only if he could hit me. As the size grew even larger, I worried I was making a mistake. Could I get out of the path of Tory's magic if Micky took it nuclear? Maybe not...

...but then fate stepped in. Not the Keeper of Fate. No, this time, fate had three names. Names I would never forget for the rest of my existence.

"NO, you impertinent beslubbering, hedge pig!" Lura Belle screeched at a decibel so high-pitched I winced.

"I will castrate you with my teeth, you haggard fat-kidneyed moldwarp!" Jolly Sue roared.

"If you throw that sparkle ball, I'll shove your salami down your throat after I rip it off with my TEETH, you mangled, boil-brained canker-blossom!" Dimple shouted.

"We will save you, Daisy," Lura Belle shouted as they got closer.

"You saved us. We will save you," Dimple insisted.

"NO," I shouted, my eyes still on Micky Muggles. "GO BACK. NOW." What were they doing on the field? They'd left with the others. They shouldn't be here in the line of fire.

"There's no going back," Jolly Sue caterwauled. "We were meant to masticate the man-meat and save you."

I watched in horror as the ball directed straight at me left the Dragon's hands. I wasn't going to be able to sprint away. Both the silver orb of destructive magic and the Nephilim were coming right at me. The magic ball came at the front, and the Nephilim came at my left. My decision to go right was not happening. I'd go left and knock the women out of the line of fire along with myself. My odds were now at about fifty-fifty. I made the decision in a split second. I didn't have time to come up with an alternative.

There was just one problem—a deadly one. The gals and the ball of Immortal-killing light were far faster than I'd anticipated. I was tackled by the three sisters and thrown about thirty feet. The gifts given to the old gals by my Angel siblings were still very obviously in their system. They shouldn't have been able to throw me even two feet.

The crazy old Nephilim high-fived each other and blew me kisses.

"No, no, no, no, NO," I shouted as I watched in horror as the ball changed direction like a heat-seeking missile programmed to find the hottest Angel of Mercy on the field. In other words, it was coming right at me.

Only I wasn't alone. The three sisters were still in range of the weapon of magical destruction, and Gideon had run to my side. Shit. We'd all die if that sucker's aim was true. The crazy, wonderful Nephilim would be no more, and my daughter would be an orphan. "No, no, no," I said again. "This can't happen."

"Fuck," Gideon hissed as he grabbed my arm. "Fly Daisy. We have to fly."

I met his gaze for the first time since I'd entered the fight, and his love gave me wings. "Go," I told him. "I have to save them." I leapt off the ground like my life depended on it, which it did, and flew at the crazy old women with one purpose: to whisk them and myself away from certain death.

I screamed when Gideon snatched me away a millisecond before the energy orb ripped through the sisters.

Too late. I'd been too late.

Gideon flew us up so high, I got light-headed. My anguish multiplied as the blueish silver ball's explosion sounded like it was coming from inside my head. The ringing in my ears was deafening. This wasn't supposed to happen.

Panic, fear, then more panic consumed me as the blinding light below me tore the old women apart. The ball turned into a vicious funnel spewing silver sparkles and blue fire. The magical tornado sucked the trio in and wouldn't let them go. It was fast, furious then over. The funnel disappeared with a burst of silver glitter. There was no trace of the fireball that had just snuffed out the lives of my friends. There was no trace of the nutty, brave women at all.

How had we gotten to this point?

Why hadn't the Nephilim left with everyone else? I'd ordered them to leave.

They hadn't listened.

And they'd paid the ultimate price.

Jolly Sue, Lura Belle and Dimple. Names I would never forget for the rest of my existence.

They had died in my place trying to save me.

My shock turned to fury as I hovered in the air with Gideon by my side. Pulling the dagger from my pants, I zoned in on the bastard who had only moments left to live. I would not be merciful. His death would be filled with the same pain now shooting through my body at the loss of Jolly Sue, Lura Belle and Dimple.

I was going to make him hurt.

Tory and Gabe strode out from behind the tree. They clearly had the same idea as me. Gabe's wings were on display. His eyes burned a bright and angry gold. Tory was still not herself, but her rage was evident. Her silver hair blew around her head, and her eyes shimmered in barely suppressed hatred. The Dragon King was spent. He was unaware that anyone was behind him. Micky Muggles' beady eyes were sunken, and he just stared in shock where the Nephilim had been only minutes ago. His magic was hanging on by a thread.

He was the one who had fucked around, and now, he was about to find out.

I landed in front of the platform. Gideon arrived by my side and placed a comforting hand on my back. My tears wouldn't stop. My heart felt broken in half. I watched as Tory viciously kicked the feet out from under Micky Muggles. He hit the ground like a sack of potatoes and whimpered like a coward. She dragged him by his hair and yanked him to his knees.

Shoving his naked, disgusting body toward the guillotine,

she made sure his *tail* was where her neck had been not very long ago. Her smile was so cold I shivered. Her pale hands were around Micky's neck—her nails digging in and drawing blood. Gabe was with her all the way.

I stayed back. The Archangel Gabriel and Purgatory deserved to take the lead. The damage he had done to both of them was repulsive.

"Shall I lock the blade?" Gabe asked Tory with his knee firmly in Micky's back so he couldn't move away. "We wouldn't want to miss."

"Please do," she said emotionlessly. "It would be a damned shame to have to castrate him twice."

"No," Micky begged in a shrill voice. "Let me leave. Don't kill me. I won't bother none of y'all no more. I swear it. Didn't mean to kill them old ladies. It was their own fault. They got in the way. Stupid bitches."

"Shut your filthy mouth," Tory snarled. "The castration won't kill you. You've lived on borrowed time at the expense of others for centuries. You murdered shamelessly... over and over. What little magic you have left is stolen. It's not yours. It was never yours."

"I won't drink no more blood," he whimpered. "I learned my lesson."

Purgatory squeezed harder. Micky's eyes began to bulge. I felt no compassion for the man.

"Hardly," Gabe ground out through clenched teeth.

The golden glow around my brother and the silver around Tory wove together and became almost too brilliant to observe. They'd both suffered for thousands of years at Zadkiel's hand, and just when they had the chance to live without sadistic abuse, Micky Muggles had come into the picture.

"I'm sorry," Micky choked out. "I ask forgiveness. You're a goddamned Angel. You ain't got no choice. You gotta forgive a sorry man."

"What are you sorry for?" Gabe demanded. "Tell me what you crave forgiveness for?"

The Dragon King's pea brain couldn't come up with anything. His mouth moved spastically but no words came out.

"There is nowhere you can hide in this Universe that will shield you from the memories of the heinous acts you've committed. Even in death, you'll never escape it. The insidious cancer of your existence will eat you until there's nothing left. Your repentance is fueled by the terror of knowing you're about to suffer the consequences of your crimes. Here's what I will give to you." The Archangel Gabriel squatted down and got in the evil man's face. "I give you my word that none of us will kill you."

"Ohhh, glory be," Micky shouted, nodding and sobbing. "Glory be!"

The Angel grabbed him by the hair. He smiled at Micky Muggles. It was terrifying. I took a small step back. Even the Grim Reaper backed away a bit. The man with his tail in the guillotine paled to the point that he looked dead.

"We don't have to kill you," Gabe explained in an icy tone. "Your greed and perverted misdeeds over the last thousand years will do it for us."

"I don't understand," Micky blubbered. "I don't get it. Not understanding. You gotta help a guy out. Come on now. Come on. Don't the Bible say somethin' about fuckin' up is human and forgiveness is in the line?"

"Divine," Tory corrected the fool.

"Right. Divine," Micky grunted trying to stand up. "So are we all good now? I can go?"

I laughed. The sound was slightly unhinged but I couldn't help myself. The piece of shit who tried repeatedly to murder everyone I loved and had been murdering for a thousand years to extend his life now thought we were *all good.* The word idiot didn't even come close to describing him. He was a delusional psychopath.

Expending little effort, Gabe pushed the self-proclaimed King back down into his favorite form of punishment. The Dragon's tail was on the block. Purgatory made sure the murdering ass didn't move.

Gabe reached up and fastened the latch on the razor-sharp blade. The click was the most satisfying sound I'd ever heard. Swiping at the tears pouring hot down my face, I realized I wasn't standing alone. Gideon was beside me, and all around us were people we loved. Tim, Candy Vargo, Dirk, Fred, Wally and Carl had joined us to watch the slaying of the dragon.

It was a visceral and heartbreaking punch to the gut to think about who was missing.

"Would you like the honors, Purgatory?" Gabe inquired, pointing to the pully that would drop the blade.

"I would, Archangel Gabriel," she replied as Micky began to scream and swear. He was ignored. "But I could use a hand."

Gabe crossed to Tory, looked deep into her eyes then took her hand in his. Together, they reached for the pully and yanked on it. The shriek of horror from the Dragon as his tail was sliced from his body made me feel nothing—no empathy, no pity, no concern... nothing.

The means to ending Micky Muggles was anticlimactic... and gross in an academic way. Gabe had stayed true to his word. None of us killed Micky Muggles, but his death came anyway. Watching it felt as if I was trapped in a B-horror flick with outstanding special effects.

Without his tail, the magic was gone. Not a trace of it was left in his pathetic and evil body. His hair turned white immediately and began to shed. He was bald within thirty seconds. His skin puckered and popped as deep grooves and lines appeared. The man's frame shrunk and his bones cracked with the brittleness of old age. Brown spots peppered his dried-out and papery husk of skin as he moaned in agony.

No one said a word. We silently watched the man who had terrorized us and so many others fall apart. He was moving quickly from borrowed time to real age.

His ears and nose grew as his eye sockets sunk in as if they'd been punched violently. Fingernails and toenails grew thick and yellow. Micky Muggles wailed as he watched his body become unrecognizable. While it appeared to be agonizing, I was unmoved. Tory was correct. The horrid man had been living for centuries on borrowed time at the expense of others. He was now paying the price... and it was high.

His teeth dropped out of his head and his skin began to blow away like tissue paper. It was interesting that there was very little blood. However, the process was happening so quickly, I might have missed it. Micky Muggles was close to skeletal now. His gray and decaying organs turned to mush and gushed out, leaving gooey puddles on the ground. What was left of his brain exited the party through his vacant eye sockets. His bones began to shatter. The minute they hit the ground they turned to dust.

The Dragon had been slayed in the most fitting way. The fire he thought he'd possessed had burned him in the end. All that was left was a pile of dust.

Candy Vargo stepped forward and waved her hand the way Gideon had done earlier with the Demons we'd slayed. The wind picked up Micky Muggles' remnants and blew them away forever. The mood was somber—not because Micky Muggles met his long-overdue demise, but because we'd lost three of the most wonderfully nutty and courageous women who had even been created.

I wasn't sure how much time they would've had left in this world. Lura Belle, Jolly Sue and Dimple were Nephilim and well into their hundredth year. But even if they'd only had a few years left, they would have been years worth living. Micky Muggles had snuffed out their candles before their time.

Tory made her way off the platform with Gabe's help. The silver-haired Angel of Purgatory walked over and embraced me. It was the first time she'd willingly shown affection, and I accepted it gladly.

The hug was too much for the rest of our crew to handle. So, they joined us. It was one big Immortal group hug, and it was needed. The rumble beneath our feet ended our cuddle party. The Tower of London was disappearing, ancient stone by ancient stone. In its place, the Kentucky Castle was taking back its rightful home.

"Friends," Tim announced. "I think it's time to go. I'd suggest sooner rather than later. Transporting seems to be in order."

"Absolutely darling," Dirk agreed. "But what about Jennifer? We can't leave her here. She might end up wasted at her sorority house again. She might end up in jail. Or worse, Goddess forbid, married again after a bender!"

"Not to worry," Tim said with a chuckle. "I shall drive back to the Airbnb and collect her. I'll transport Jennifer, the mail truck, the minivan and myself back to Georgia."

"What about our steeds?" Wally asked.

"Umm… you're on your own with that," Tim told him.

"Fair enough," Wally said, extending his hands as Tim hustled back to the minivan. "Shall we?"

"Yes, we fuckin' shall," Candy Vargo said. "And in the words of the piece of shit whose dick we just lopped off…" She turned and faced the spot where Micky Muggles had disintegrated. "See ya. Wouldn't wanna be ya."

It was time to go home.

In a blast of shimmering magic, we left the castle.

CHAPTER TEN

After two days where pretty much all I did was hold my baby and weep for the Nephilim we'd lost, I knew I'd have to rejoin the world of the living. Gideon had been by my side every moment, allowing me to grieve at my own pace. I didn't think I could love him more than I already did, but he was like a beautiful gift that just kept on giving.

Thankfully, everyone and everything at home was good. Tim had successfully transported Jennifer and the vehicles. We'd made it back in one piece with the horses in tow. Gram and Mr. Jackson had managed to lead the three hundred ghosts back to my home. Her history as the Death Counselor made her the perfect escort. Even so, with the thirty deceased guests already living here, we had a full house.

My siblings offered to host a hundred and fifty at my old farmhouse until I could make the time to help all of them crossover. From what I understood during my brief chat with the ghost Gragraunch, they'd been trapped in the Tower of London for a long time—some had been there for centuries. I still couldn't fathom how the ancient fortress had been relocated to Lexington, Kentucky. My mind knew that magic wasn't always logical, but it was still difficult to wrap my head around. Crazily enough, the ghosts were thrilled to be in our sleepy little Georgia town, and seemed well-adjusted for what they'd been through. Plus, they adored my baby. That made them welcome in my book. The warmth they held for Alana Catherine was reciprocated by my child. She giggled like a loon when our dead friends popped up to ooo and ahh over her.

The gift had not skipped a generation. Sometime in the distant future, my daughter would take over for me as the Death Counselor. Right now, the dead were just her playmates. I wasn't sure how I felt about her taking over the responsibility when she got older, but as her mom, I was working with what I was given.

We'd held a remembrance ceremony for Lura Belle, Jolly Sue and Dimple under my favorite tree in the front yard. We were having a week of gorgeous weather in the middle of winter. Everyone wore conservative Chanel pantsuits and sensible shoes—even the men. It was fitting. I don't know how, but Gideon had made his powder blue suit with the floral lapel look sexy.

The sun shone bright in the sky as we talked about the old gals. It was kind of difficult to find stories where they hadn't been colossal bitches since they'd only become socially acceptable recently, but Candy Vargo had everyone roaring with laughter at a few of the less offensive stories from the sisters' pasts. Tim had whipped up the gals' go-to snack—sweet tea, hot biscuits and creamed peas. Gross didn't begin cover it, but I indulged a little in their honor.

I'd secretly hoped they would show up as ghosts, but Tory had quashed that desire. The vortex had destroyed them—

souls and all. If I thought about it too hard, I felt ill. I had to be satisfied that, in the end, they knew they were loved and respected.

Since I couldn't have Jolly Sue, Lura Belle and Dimple back as ghosts, I'd focus on the ones who were here. There were tons of dead in-residence with missing body parts. I had the superglue and know-how to put them back together. Tomorrow would be a new day filled with promise and joy.

It was time to get back to work.

"Sugar Pants!" Wally squealed. He sashayed into the living room at seven AM while I was breastfeeding Alana Catherine.

She'd slept through the night and was chipper and starving when she woke. I was happy to be her cow. It was an honor. Her milk-drunk expression as she stared at me was humbling. It had become my new favorite thing.

Wally cat-walked and posed around the room like it was his personal runway. "It's a glorious day, and we're having an eleganza extravaganza!" He popped his tongue when he finished.

I was confused. I assumed he was talking about a party of some kind, but I wasn't sure what he wanted to celebrate. "For the Nephilim?" We'd commemorated them yesterday, but if my friends wanted to do it again, I was in.

"Ohhhhhhh no, snookums," he said with a silly grin as he waggled his perfectly plucked eyebrows. "Something more life-affirming."

"Such as?" I questioned, hoping it wasn't a karaoke party. The queens loved to sing, but they were tone deaf.

"It's a surprise," he said, twirling and showing off his to-die-for ruby-sequined Prada gown.

"For?" I asked, getting more suspicious by the second. It was seriously early in the day for Prada.

"If I tell you, it won't be a surprise. Come with me. We need to get you gussied up. You're a hot mess."

"Umm... thanks," I muttered with a laugh as I brushed baby spit-up off my shirt. Wally wasn't wrong. My sweats might not match, and I was wearing Ugg boots that had seen better days, but I was feeling pretty darn good, mentally and physically. I'd showered *and* brushed my teeth. That had to count as a win, right? On top of all that, for the first time in a long while, I didn't have an Immortal enemy actively trying to kill me. Yay, me. I reached over and knocked on the wooden side table to keep from jinxing myself.

June and Jennifer hustled into the room dressed up all fancy. I heard Heather, Missy and Amelia in the kitchen whispering urgently a mile a minute, but I couldn't make out a single word. My Spidey senses were tingling. Hard. Why had everyone freaking shown up at dawn's butt-crack? June wore a lovely rose-pink linen dress and strappy sandals. Jennifer was killing it in a sharp, bright-red silk suit with matching earrings and heels.

Was it someone's birthday, and I'd forgotten about it? I didn't think so... Alana Catherine was done eating, and I gently burped her. She let one rip that sounded as if it came from a full-grown man. Her squeal of delight at her gassy announcement made all of us laugh. Babies were very good medicine for a sad heart.

"Give me that adorable bundle," June said with a giggle, holding out her arms. "You need to get ready."

"For what?" I asked, handing over the best thing I'd ever made to my dear friend.

"Not tellin'," Jennifer said with a naughty grin. "Just go with it."

"As long as it doesn't involve bloodshed, I'm in," I said, following Wally up the stairs.

Dirk stood at the entrance to my bedroom with his hands on his hips and a smirk on his glossy red lips. "Prepare to surrender."

"Oh my Hell," I said with a laugh as I was yanked into the bedroom by four giddy queens.

"OH MY GOD," I WHISPERED AS I LOOKED IN THE MIRROR. "Is that me?"

"Sure is, Girlfriend!" Fred gushed as he examined his handiwork. "Gorgeous."

"Werk it," Wally added with another tongue pop and a finger snap that made me laugh.

For the last two hours, I'd been scrubbed, massaged, face-masked, waxed, brushed, plucked, painted and primped. My bedroom had turned into a spa on crack. My buddies were on a roll. The squealing was real. Theirs, not mine. I still wasn't sure what was going on. They'd put sheets over the mirrors so the results would be a surprise. After thirty minutes of having makeup applied by Dirk, I was worried I'd end up looking like a hooker.

I did not. I knew I could clean up well, but the queens raised the bar. The queens had done my makeup tastefully but full of glamour. And my brows...damn, they were on point and flawless. I felt like a dang supermodel and was ready for my close-up.

"I am sooooo jealous, Hot Pants!" Carl cried out, brushing a tear from his eye. "You're positively stunning. That mug is beat for the gods! Dirk, you've outdone yourself."

The Horseman, known as Death, took a bow.

"How do you like your hair, gal pal?" Fred asked, excitedly bouncing on his stiletto-clad toes.

Fred had spent even more time on my wild, curly, dark hair. He'd swept it into an up-do, finishing the style with wispy tendrils that framed my face. After, he'd woven in sparkling crystals that shimmered and peeked out from underneath my curls.

"I feel like a princess," I whispered, squeezing his hand.

Fred preened then danced around the room, flapping his long muscular arms like he was a chicken.

"Ohhhhhhh, you're bad," Dirk shouted at Fred. "Don't give her any hints about the extravaganza yet."

Fred's peal of laughter made me laugh. Of course, I had no clue as to why. What kind of hint was a dancing chicken? Did they buy—or rather steal—a chicken coop for me? Shit. That would suck. That couldn't be the reason for a party.

"It's fine," I told Dirk. "I don't understand the clue."

"Not to worry," Carl said, running to my closet. "You will soon."

"You know, darling," Fred announced as he sat down at the vanity next to me and reapplied his lipstick. "I'm feeling quite punny on this fine day. Shall we have some pun?"

"You mean fun?" I asked, in awe of his lipstick prowess.

"Nope," he said with a wink. "I mean pun."

"Oh yes!" Carl yelled from my closet. "It's a punderful life, and I say we celebrate it."

I groaned. They laughed and kept going.

"It's quite a difficult pun-dertaking, but I'm up for it," Dirk said with a wicked chuckle. "However, this is the pun-house."

My second groan was louder, and it only served to egg them on.

"I've got one," Carl said, popping his head out of the closet. "What's the best part of a wedding?" He didn't wait for an answer. "The reception. It usually takes the cake!"

"Nice," Wally told his fellow Horseman. "Did you know the lucky couple that hired a fabu vegetarian DJ for the reception? It was because he could really turnip the beets!"

Dirk plopped down on the bed and grinned at me. "I heard the couple were both pianists. They were always in a chord."

I squinted at him. I might be wrong, but I thought I was catching on. However, not a word left my lips. It would be mortifying if I was incorrect.

"If we're talking music…" Wally watched me carefully. The nutbag was cheesing from ear to ear. "When the famous musician proposed to the love of his life, he did it with a kneel diamond."

My mouth fell open. I was positive I was onto them, but still too terrified to say it.

The puns were flying fast and furious.

"I heard the dentist had strong fillings for his new spouse," Carl said.

Wally jumped in. "For butter or worse! A toast to the newlyweds!"

"I hear vampire weddings really suck," Dirk added with a waggle of his brows.

"Yes, well," Fred said with a shimmy and a jazz square. "Marrying in July is very brave, for the personal trainer couple, but what can you expect from sweat-hearts?"

Carl would not be outdone. "Now that they're married, they're both footloose and fiancé free!"

I realized I was trembling. Not from fear, but with excitement. "Wait. Stop. I want to take a guess."

"It's about time, Girlfriend," Wally said.

"Am I..." I started, then paused. If I was wrong, it would be embarrassing. However, I didn't think I was. "Umm... is the party a ceremony of sorts? A binding one?"

All four queens looked like kids on Christmas morning. "Yes," they said at the same time.

"Is it something you do once?"

Fred pursed his lips then squeaked. "Hopefully, yes. But if you're Jennifer... then, no."

"You are soooo bad at throwing that shade," Carl chastised Fred. He pretended to take off glasses and set them down. "You can't read your way out of a paper bag. The library is officially closed."

"My fantabulous Jennifer would've laughed," Fred shot back.

He was correct. Actually, Jennifer would have made that exact joke.

I had a few more things I wanted clarified. "And umm... is this something most of the guests sit down for?"

"Yes," Dirk said, barely holding back a scream. "Of course, there are people who stand."

"In the front," Wally said.

"With an officiant," Carl added, coming fully out of my closet with a garment bag in hand. "Who hopefully uses the F-bomb sparingly."

The boys didn't need to scream. I did it for them. "Am I getting married?"

"Surprise!" they yelled in unison.

Again, I screamed. This time they joined me.

I grabbed a tissue and dabbed at my eyes. I didn't want to ruin my makeup.

"Waterproof mascara," Dirk assured me as he grabbed a handful of tissue and passed them around. "Cry all you want, Babycakes. It's your party."

An alarming thought occurred to me. "Does Gideon know?"

Fred dabbed his eyes, and then blew his nose. "I would assume by now he does. Charlie, Tim, Gabe, Zander and Rafe are with him. They've been tasked with getting your hot hunk of love into a tuxedo. The Grim Reaper isn't a dim man. He knows!"

The Chicken Dance now made sense. It was an obscure hint, but it was a hint.

"And you don't need to worry about a thing," Dirk said, pulling me to my feet. "We've done it all. It's the first wedding we've hosted, and it's going to be slay!"

"Define slay," I said, eyeing the garment bag. I crossed my fingers and hoped it wasn't blinged out like a drag show costume. Sequins weren't my thing.

Wally pulled a piece of paper from his cleavage. "Here's the song list! You'll walk down the aisle to *Every Breath You Take*."

I wanted to point out that it was basically a stalker song, but refrained. They were too excited, and I didn't want to kill the vibe.

"Oh! And Gideon will walk down the aisle to *Y.M.C.A.*," Wally added.

I pressed my lips together. It was abundantly clear they'd never been to a wedding before. I was wildly curious but mostly terrified to hear the rest. They didn't disappoint. The theme song from *Rocky, Back In Black, Macarena,* and, of course, the *Chicken Dance* were on the list.

Whatever. It would be a story to tell for centuries.

"Are you ready to see your dress?" Carl inquired, about to burst his seams.

"I am."

The boys might not know much about weddings, but they did know dresses. It was a strapless champagne-colored masterpiece. A little crystal beading here and there to match the jewels in my hair. The Manolo Blahnik peep-toed stilettos went with the dress perfectly. I couldn't have picked a more gorgeous dress myself.

"You likey?" Dirk asked cautiously.

"I lovey," I replied, dabbing at my eyes again.

He let out a squeal of triumphant joy. "I knew you would. I feel like a grand fairy godmother."

"And a wonderful one at that," I told him, still misty-eyed. I glanced around at my four fabulous friends, my heart bursting with love for them. My voice was hoarse with emotion. "You're all so wonderful. Thank you. This. All of this has made me so happy. Marrying Gideon is the only thing that could possibly make me happier."

"Then I say we get you dressed and down the aisle," Carl said, sobbing happy tears.

Dirk, Fred and Wally joined him. The five of us were a sight to behold, crying and laughing as they fit me into my gown.

It was a damned good thing Dirk had used waterproof mascara.

CHAPTER ELEVEN

I STOOD ON THE FRONT PORCH OF THE HOUSE GIDEON AND I HAD created together with love and gazed out over the yard in shock. My tummy flipped, but it wasn't from fear or stress. It was from giddiness and joy. Normally, the yard was grass and trees. Today, it was not.

Someone, or a bunch of someones, had converted our property into an exquisite garden. It was pure magic. Candles hung overhead in the air, floating on a gentle and fragrant breeze. Scattered peach and pale-pink rose petals created a path leading to a gazebo covered in vines bursting with white, cream and dusty rose-colored blossoms. Flowers and ornamental grasses swayed in the light wind while the clouds in the sky appeared larger and puffier. Flocks of wildly colored birds darted in and out of the trees and the winter sun bathed the entire picture in a warm golden glow.

"Oh my," I whispered, taking it all in with delight. June had given me some solid advice ten minutes earlier as I'd waited in the foyer for the wedding to begin.

"Once the dress is on, don't worry about it getting messed

up," she said sagely. "It will at some point and who cares? Listen to the ceremony, and don't get wasted at the reception."

They were logical and smart pointers, just like my buddy June. I added one more thought to the list—take in the beauty around me and treasure it.

"You look so lovely, Daisy girl," Gram said as she hovered next to me. "Lemme tell you, I'm so dang excited to walk my baby down the aisle, I think my head might fall off! Kiddin'!" she added to my relief. Having to superglue Gram's head back on during the wedding march might kill some of the romantic atmosphere. The old ghost chuckled and then gazed at me fondly. "You bein' happy just dills my pickles. You look as fine as a frog hair split four ways."

I giggled. Gram was being vintage Gram. "I love you and thank you."

"For what?" she asked, caressing my cheek with her papery hand.

"For loving me. For raising me. For staying with me," I said, pulling out a tissue and putting it to good use. "And for walking me down the aisle."

"Pleasure is all mine, baby girl," she told me. "All mine."

Dabbing at my eyes so I didn't have a streaky, tear-stained face, I gazed at the stunning picture in front of me. There were several rows of seating. Everyone was here—Heather and Missy held hands and leaned into each other the way people who loved each other did. Tim, Jennifer, June and Charlie sat together. June held a sleepy Alana Catherine on her lap, and my fur babies, Donna and Karen lay on the ground at her feet. Charlie's arm was draped over June's shoulders, and Jennifer, with a bottle of wine in hand, cooed at my baby. As my friend liked to say… it was five o'clock somewhere. Tim, dapper in his mail uniform, had added a bow tie and a top hat to his look. It was a massive fashion faux pas—so wrong it was absolutely right. Instead of a notebook and pen, today, my socially awkward buddy had a camera and was snapping pictures. I knew this day would stay in my heart and my memories, but it would be lovely to have physical reminders.

Zander and his sister Catriona sat with my Angel siblings—Rafe, Gabe, Abby and Prue. Tory and Amelia rounded out the group. Amelia sat next to Rafe and their connection was undeniable. The energy around them was electric. Everyone was dressed to the nines and looked like they'd stepped off the cover of a magazine. Zander couldn't take his eyes off of Prue. She studiously ignored him, of course, but the small smile pulling at her lips was a dead giveaway that she was into it. There was a story developing there, and I had my fingers crossed for a happily ever after. However, the biggest story of that grouping was Gabe and Tory. Tory no longer denied her feelings for my brother. They were taking it slow, but they had an eternity to get it right. Both of them were glowing... literally.

Their love story had been thousands of years in the making, and I had a feeling it was about to unfold into a beautiful ending.

"It's almost time," Gram said softly. "You ready?"

"More ready than I've ever been," I told her with a smile so wide it hurt my cheeks. "Where's Gideon?"

"He'll be coming out with Candy Vargo in just a sec," she told me. "That boy has it bad for you. He's been walking around grinnin' like a possum eatin' a sweet tater!"

"That makes two of us," I said with a laugh.

The Four Horsemen of the Apocalypse were running the show. Dirk seated the last of the guests. Wally coordinated all the music—which was kind of alarming, considering the playlist, but nothing would ruin this day, even cringy inappropriate songs. Fred traipsed up and down the aisle, offering flutes of champagne. Most everyone accepted a glass. Jennifer took two. Carl stood next to the gazebo, looking fabulous, and posed for the camera. Tim obliged and took plenty of pics.

Mr. Jackson and my three hundred or so other dead guests were in attendance as well. They might have been more excited for the ceremony than I was. The ghosts darted around and chattered with rabid excitement. There were a few random body parts lying around. Didn't matter. It was par for the course in my life, and I'd deal with it after the ceremony. It was macabre, beautiful and very, very right. I wore many hats, mom, soon to be wife, sister, granddaughter, friend, Angel of Mercy, badass and Death Counselor. It was perfect that my people were all here.

Candy Vargo appeared on the platform of the gazebo in a blast of sparkling orange mist. The guests applauded her showmanship. She bowed and tossed boxes of toothpicks to the crowd. I almost choked on my spit at the outfit she wore. She wore a magnificent gold Prada sheath dress that was simple in design and gorgeous in reality. Of course, she paired it with shitty tennis shoes and a toothpick hanging out of her mouth, but Candy was Candy and that wasn't ever going to change. The queens had dressed her—everything except the shoes and the toothpick accessory. I was sure of that. When her gaze met mine, she smiled, waved, and then flipped me off.

I returned the gesture, and she cackled like an idiot.

"You ready, asshead?" she yelled.

"I'm ready, butthole," I yelled back.

"Then let's get this fuckin' party started!"

"Watch that mouth," Gram told her, giving her the stink-eye.

The Keeper of Fate blanched and gave Gram a thumbs up. I didn't believe Candy Vargo was capable of watching her mouth. Honestly, I didn't want her to. It wouldn't be a party without Candy dropping a few F-bombs.

"Oh my!" Dirk squealed as Gideon walked onto the gazebo. "You are hotter than Satan's underpants, if he existed, which he doesn't, but I'm sticking with my story!"

Dirk was correct. My heart skipped a beat, and my mouth went dry when our eyes met. The man of my dreams gazed at me with love and desire in his eyes. It made me forget for a moment that we weren't the only people here. It was humbling to the point that I thought I might faint. The smile pulling at the corner of his kissable lips promised a lifetime of adventure. I was all in.

"All right, people," Candy shouted. "Get your asses up. You gotta stand when the bride walks down the aisle."

The people listened.

"Lookin' like it's our turn," Gram said.

"Lookin' like it is," I agreed.

"Music," Candy Vargo ordered, pointing her chewed-up toothpick at Wally.

"On it, Doll Face!" Wally pushed the button, and Sting's voice came through the speakers. *Every Breath You Take* blasted loud and proud.

A few of the guests winced at the song choice, but I just shook my head and went with it. Nothing could ruin my day. I would have loved for my mom and dad to be here, but that wasn't possible. I was thrilled at the gathering assembled. It included my nearest and dearest.

The melody of the song was beautiful even if the words were kind of creepy. I felt the strong impulse to run to Gideon, tackle him and play tonsil hockey, but thankfully Gram had tucked her ghostly arm through mine. Literally. She floated at a slower pace which was far more appropriate. It would have been a major faux pas for me to sprint down the aisle dragging my dead grandmother, but it was exactly what I wanted to do.

Gideon's eyes burned red with love and adoration as I approached. Gram handed me over and booped the Grim Reaper's nose before she floated away, seating herself next to Heather and Missy.

"Stunning," Gideon whispered.

"Back at ya, Sexy Pants," I said. "You okay with this? I mean, it seems kind of shotgun."

He threw his head back and laughed. It filled my soul.

Gideon in a tux should be illegal. He was more beautiful than any movie star or model from a magazine. But even more important than his fine abs, ass, kissable lips and other things I shouldn't think about while our families, friends and daughter were present, was his heart. It was kind, strong, loving and good. And it was mine.

"It's my fuckin' turn," Candy Vargo announced, pulling out a toothpick box that she had turned into a cheat sheet.

"Let's try to keep the profanity to a minimum," Tim suggested.

"Will do. Jackasses, did you hear the mailman?" she demanded of Gideon and me with a cackle.

"Pretty sure he was talking to you," I shot back.

"Hmm…" She considered the possibility and then shrugged. "You ready for me to marry you two?"

"Do we have a choice?" I asked with an answering grin.

"Nope."

"Then we're ready," Gideon said.

"Did either of you happen to write your fuckin' vows?" Candy Vargo inquired.

"Watch that mouth, girlie, or I'm gonna tie your tongue in a knot," Gram shouted.

"My bad," Candy answered her with a wave. She refocused on us. "So? Vows?"

I squinted at her in disbelief. "Are you serious? Neither one of us even knew we were getting married this afternoon. Why would you think we'd have written our own vows?

"Relax your fuckin' sphincter crack," Candy said. "You can just pull 'em out of your ass."

"Candy Vargo," Gram called out, waggling her finger.

"Whoops," Candy said. "I meant to say, relax your fornicating gluteal muscles."

"Lordy have mercy," Gram choked out on a laugh. "I ain't sure that's much better. But at least it wasn't an F-bomb."

"Say what's in your heart," Heather said.

"Grand idea," Fred agreed.

My sister was right. She was usually right. However, I needed someone else with us to do it correctly. I held up a finger to Gideon, who seemed a bit confused. Hustling over to June, I held out my arms for my baby. In order to marry Gideon, we needed our entire little family together. With our child cradled to my chest, I walked back to the man I wanted to spend my long life with. His smile was what I expected. The happy tears in his eyes, I did not. For a Demon, the guy was in touch with his emotions. He was a keeper.

He pulled us close and whispered in my ear. "Say your vows, Counselor."

"Getting there, Reaper," I replied as Alana Catherine reached up and pulled his hair with a giggle that made my waterworks turn on. I inhaled deeply and blew it out slowly. Speaking from my heart was easy. I was so filled with love I just let it rip. "Gideon, you're the love of my life—my best friend. I promise you this, every day I will cherish you. I will love you. I will laugh and cry with you. I'll be by your side to kick ass when necessary, which I hope we get a break from for a little while." The crowd laughed. They got it. We all needed a freaking break. "I'm your ride or die, and you're mine. I don't know what I did in my life to get so lucky, but I'm thankful for it with all of my heart. Together, we'll have a home full of love for our daughter, and I want to live each day of our seriously long lives with you by my side. I promise to be your partner, lover and bestie until the end of time. My life truly started the day I met you."

Gideon's grin set my thong on fire, and the kiss he planted on my lips made my head spin.

"Keep your tongue in your mouth, boy," Candy grunted, slapping the Grim Reaper on the back of the head. "You need to pull some vows out of your ass, and then I'll say the man and wife shit." She checked her notes on the toothpick box. "After that, you can go on up to your room and bang. Got it?"

"Got it," Gideon said with a wince and a chuckle. He turned his attention to me and got very serious. "Daisy, my life started when you came into it. You make it worth living and even though I didn't know it, I'd been waiting an eternity for you. Literally." His lopsided grin made my knees weak. "It wasn't until you came into my life that I truly understood what love meant. You and Alana Catherine are the reasons for each and every breath I take." He paused and chuckled. "Kind of like the stalker song that was played when you walked down the aisle."

I laughed. Hard. The queens didn't. They were wildly confused.

"That being said," Gideon continued. "I promise to be your husband, best friend, lover and partner in juicy boner justice until the end of time." I giggled, and he grinned. "I promise to love, cherish and worship you and our daughter. I will protect you with my life… because my existence would be meaningless without you. I love you."

"Love you more," I whispered.

"Not possible," he shot back.

"You done, fucker?" Candy Vargo asked Gideon.

"For the love of everything you ain't supposed to say at a wedding," Gram grumbled. "Candy Vargo, you're makin' my rump itch. I swear I'm gonna jerk you bald if you don't control that potty mouth."

"Will do, Gram," Candy said, blanching. Only Gram could put the Keeper of Fate in her place without being electrocuted. Gram might be dead, but she still ruled the roost.

"Yes, I'm done," Gideon said.

"Okay then, by the power vested in me because I took an online crash course in officiating weddings, I now pronounce you husband and wife. You can now stick your tongue down Daisy's throat or go on upstairs and bang. However, it is rather obvious you've had premarital sex due to the bundle of joy in your hands…" She waved a hand in front of her face and wrinkled her nose. "Who may or may not have just pooped her pants."

It wasn't a typical wedding, but we weren't typical. And Candy was correct. Alana Catherine had just dropped a few friends off at the lake. It would be dealt with shortly. But it could wait a minute. Now, it was time for a lip lock with my *husband.*

Gideon leaned in and kissed me.

I kissed him right back.

The deal was sealed, and nothing in the world could make me happier.

CHAPTER TWELVE

GIDEON AND I WERE COMMANDED TO TAKE A QUICK BREAK TO change clothes for the reception. The queens, with naughty expressions on their faces, insisted they needed an hour to set up the finale of the extravaganza. Heather and Missy took Alana Catherine for a diaper change and stroller ride. Candy Vargo mentioned the banging part of the vows again and only stopped pontificating about it when Gram threatened to cancel her birth certificate. Everyone else tried to hide their grins and pretend they had no clue what was going on.

They failed and were fooling no one.

We were fooling no one as we casually walked back into the house then raced up the stairs to our bedroom like horny teenagers.

"We've got an hour," Gideon said, tearing his tux off and tossing it aside. He made quick work of my gown before throwing me onto the bed. "Let's not waste a second of it."

"Deal," I said, as he fell onto the bed next to me. I climbed on top of him, straddling my man and smiling so hard my face hurt.

Stuff was about to get sweaty, sexy and good. We were both a hundred thousand percent committed. The odds were excellent for an orgasmic time.

~

"HOLY HELL," GIDEON SAID WITH AN EXHAUSTED LAUGH AS HE pulled me in to a hug and kissed the top of my head.

My hair was no longer in a lovely upswept do. It was wild—as wild as the sex we'd had for the past hour. Our bed looked like a tornado had hit it, and I'd been kind of worried our friends and family might hear us. Whatever. I'd ceased to care about that after the first earthquake-inducing orgasm.

"This might sound insane, but I think married sex beats single sex." I traced his full lips with my finger.

"I'm inclined to agree," he said with the grin of a very satiated man. "But maybe we should go another round to make sure."

I rolled over and checked my watch. "Can't. We'll be late to our own reception. You think four times wasn't enough?"

He raised a brow and gave me a *look*. All he had to do was rake me over with his gorgeous eyes, and I was ready to go. Orgasms with my husband were beyond awesome. Like Lays Potato Chips... one, or four in my case, was never enough.

"A hundred times wouldn't be enough," he informed me in a voice so sexy, I considered taking him up on his offer.

"A hundred times in a row might kill us," I pointed out with a giggle.

"Not a problem. We're Immortal." His smile was positively feral.

I was soooo tempted, but we had an eternity to make love. And we would take full advantage of that lovely fact.

"Fine point. Well made," I said, reluctantly slipping out of his embrace and grabbing the dress the queens had provided for the reception. "However, we have an elegaaanza extrava-gaaaanza," I elongated the words, mimicking the queens for dramatic effect, "to go to, and I want to dance with my husband and daughter. Plus, I'm pretty sure if we're late, Candy Vargo will come up here and drag us to the party naked."

"There's a visual that just killed my libido," he said with a groan as he put his tux back on.

"I'm good like that," I told him, stepping into the amazing Prada wedges that went perfectly with the Marchesa gown the boys had chosen. While sequins weren't normally my thing, the gown was to die for—the intricate threadwork woven in with teal sequins and floral applique was delicate and exquisite. The dress shimmered when I moved. It felt alive and magical on my body. In my wedding gown, I'd felt like a princess. In my party dress, I felt like a freaking queen. Quickly twisting my hair back up, I reapplied the lipstick that had been kissed off and was ready to rumble.

"I have a stunning wife," Gideon said, admiring me.

"And I have a sexy badass husband," I told him.

He kissed me sweetly and cupped my chin in his hand. "You happy?"

I sighed happily. I finally had everything I'd ever dreamed of and more than I could've ever imagined. I had great friends who always had my back, sisters and brothers who I cherished, my gram, my child, and the most delicious, handsome hunk of a husband that I loved more than life itself.

Our eyes met, and I told him with all sincerity, "More than I've ever thought possible."

He smiled as he wrapped his arms around me and kissed

me again. The warmth of his embrace, and the tenderness in his lips as they moved against mine nearly brought me to tears. I'd never felt so beautiful or wanted.

"I plan to make your happiness my only mission for the rest of our lives," he whispered against my lips.

"You don't even have to try to succeed at that," I said, giving him a final kiss. As much as I was enjoying the moment, we had a lifetime of them coming, and our guests, who had taken time out of their lives to celebrate us, were waiting downstairs. "You ready to party with the crazies?"

"I am," he replied, picking me up as if I weighed no more than a feather before whisking me down the stairs to the party.

It was time to get to the reception before the reception came to us.

"Let the festivities begin!" Wally shouted as Carl clapped his hands and produced a karaoke machine.

My hopes for a party without a version of *Islands in the Stream* sung in the key of X by Carl and Dirk was dashed. But I didn't care. It wouldn't be an extravaganza without karaoke sung by some tone-deaf drag queens—at least that's what Wally had said.

Food and drink had been placed on long, elaborately decorated, flower-covered tables. Tim had cooked up a storm. There were hot dishes in all varieties—even vegetarian for me. It smelled rank, but he was so proud of himself that everyone partook. Mirror balls dropped from the tree branches and the queens had removed all the chairs from the ceremony and placed them at the large round tables that had magically appeared. A temporary dance floor had been centrally located, perfect for shaking your groove thing. The dead had already started, and parts were flying off them as they flapped their arms...or what was left of their arms in some of their cases.

I shook my head at the sight.

Watching three hundred ghosts do the Chicken Dance was something I'd never in my life thought I'd see. It got even weirder when Candy Vargo started clucking and pretending to lay an egg out of her butt. At least, she was having fun. She hadn't even noticed that about a hundred specters had flown away in horror.

Glittering pink and champagne-colored balloons floated in the air much to the delight of the jubilant guests—especially our baby. Alana Catherine squealed with joy every time one floated by her. I'd never been hugged and kissed so much in my life. I held my daughter in my arms, and my *husband* stood at our side. It was every kind of wonderful.

Until it wasn't...

"What the fuck is that?" Candy Vargo shouted, pointing to the sky.

Three blindingly bright lights were headed our way. They bounced through the air clumsily and crashed into each other multiple times.

"Aliens?" Carl squawked.

"I think UFOs," Dirk squealed.

Tim immediately pulled out his notebook. He glanced up at the incoming lights then spoke. "Doesn't look like any UFO I've seen," he said. "But a total of 12,618 sightings have been recorded from 1948 until 1969. I'm quite sure the recent numbers are much higher."

"How in the fuck is that helping?" Candy demanded, tossing her toothpicks in the air, then waving her hands and arming herself like she was ready to go into battle.

"I don't know," Tim said frantically. "My go-to instinct in times of danger is reciting facts. And speaking of... did you know that thousands of Americans have taken out insurance against aliens?"

Heather rolled her eyes, her multitude of tattoos doing a war dance along her skin as she prepared for the incoming fight. "Not helping. Everyone, get in a line. If we have to, we'll destroy it. However, we need to figure out if they come in peace before we blow them up."

No, no, no, I thought. *Not on my freaking wedding day!* I'd be damned if some extraterrestrial from outer space was going to ruin my special day.

"Excellent thinking," Charlie said as his eyes went icy blue and his badass showed. "Rafe, Prue and Abby, get June, Amelia, Missy, Jennifer and Alana Catherine into the house. Gideon drop a ward around it once they're inside."

Things were getting serious. *Shit, shit, shit.*

"On it," Gideon said, ushering the humans and our child to safety.

The lights were still zig-zagging toward us, getting bigger by the second. "Ghosts," I shouted, my hands sparking like they were about to detonate. "I want you to hide. We don't know the intentions of the umm... aliens... or, whatever they are. Until we do, disappear. NOW."

In a gust of wind, the dead vanished from sight. I shook my head. Was I ever going to get a day of freaking peace? It certainly didn't seem like it.

"Ward has been dropped," Gideon said as he joined the line of defense.

I glanced over at him. "This is either going to turn out to be a great story or a shitshow. Thoughts?"

"I'm going with great story until further notice," he replied, watching the incoming lights warily. "However, if it becomes a shitshow, I'm ready."

I nodded and adjusted my expectations. "Me too."

And then something amazing happened.

Something unbelievable.

Something I didn't think was possible.

However, nothing was impossible... one just had to believe.

I squinted as the dots of light grew closer. From a distance, they had looked like balls of fire. At closer inspection... they didn't look like balls at all.

They were shaped like bodies. A surge of joy jolted through me when I recognized our incoming aliens as the ghostly bodies of three old women wearing conservative Chanel suits and sensible pumps.

"Well, I have fuckin' never," Candy Vargo shouted, tossing her sword to the ground and running toward the incoming *aliens.*

Tim joined her and waved like a madman as the gals came in for a crash landing.

"Am I seeing what I think I'm seeing?" Heather asked with a laugh. Her magical tattoos were no longer dancing menacingly over her skin. Instead, they were waltzing blissfully up and down her arms.

"Umm... yes," I said, already crying. "Gideon, drop the ward. Tell everyone to come back out. We have some late guests."

Lura Belle, Jolly Sue and Dimple were definitely dead, but they looked pretty darn good for getting torn apart and sucked into a vortex of deadly Purgatory magic.

"Hello, all you fly-bitten moldwarps," Lura Belle said with a silly smile on her normally pursed cat-butt lips. "What did we miss while we were indisposed?"

"A fuckin' wedding," Candy said.

"Unacceptable," Jolly Sue grumbled. "We've only been gone a few days, and you boil-brained, goatish canker-blossoms had a wedding without us?"

"Oh my," Dimple fretted. "It's a very haggard, fat-kidneyed hugger-mugger thing to not include us!"

I agreed. I walked over to the Nephilim and hugged each one of them. Parts of their bodies went right through mine. Still, I was able to feel them, and they could feel me. "Welcome back. Can you stay a while?"

"I have no clue," Dimple admitted. "However, we're here now. I insist the wedding be redone. It's rude not to."

I turned and looked at Gideon. He simply shrugged. "I'd marry you a thousand times over. I'm in."

"Candy? Can you pull that crap you said out of your butt again?" I asked.

"I just pulled an imaginary chicken egg out of my ass," she reminded me. "Of course, I can yank a few F-bombs out and remarry you fuckers."

I snorted. It was unavoidable. "Alrighty then. Let's get married."

"Hang on," Lura Belle said, looking up at the sky and growing increasingly uncomfortable. "We have a message."

"From who?" I asked, feeling a little wonky but unsure why.

"The Higher Power," she said.

Now I knew why I felt wonky. Not much good came via the Higher Power.

"The message?" I held my breath, waiting for the answer.

"They're coming back," Lura Belle relayed. "The balance has shifted and must be repaired. If not... it will be a problem."

I had so many questions, but I would deal with one at a time. "Who is coming back?"

"I don't know," Lura Belle admitted.

"Can you define *problem?*" I pressed, knowing it was probably futile.

Again, she didn't know.

We all stood in silence and mulled over the new wrinkle that could unravel our lives… again. Catching a break and going on vacation was looking less likely.

"Holy motherfuckin' shitballs," Candy Vargo shouted. "What the actual fuck?"

I whipped around in the direction of Candy voice and gasped. What the actual fuck was correct.

On my front porch, transparent shoulder to transparent shoulder, stood some very familiar people to me. My gut clenched and my skin turned clammy. The group was expressionless and appeared scared.

Slowly, I walked toward the porch. Gideon fell in step to my right. Charlie to my left. Candy Vargo, Tim. Tory and Heather backed up Charlie. Gabe, Rafe, Prue and Abby stayed on Gideon's side. Zander and Catriona were behind me and the Four Horsemen of the Apocalypse brought up the rear.

I wasn't terrified of what I saw, but I was worried… worried for the ones on my porch. Something had gone wrong, terribly wrong.

"Steve?" I called out.

My dead husband barely acknowledged me. It was as if he couldn't understand. He trembled and faded in and out. Standing beside him was Sam, Sister Catherine, Agnes, Birdie and John. They weren't supposed to be here. They'd gone into the Light. I'd seen them go into the Light. I'd helped them do it.

But they were back.

Agnes floated forward. She was a shell of who she'd been. The joy and vitality had been stripped from her. Her vocal rhythm was staccato and off. Her words were even worse. "Fix the rift in the chain, Angel of Mercy. If unattended, evil from the Darkness will descend on the earth and tear it open for good. Death and destruction will rule."

"How?" I asked, hoping for more... a clue, a hint. I didn't even care if it was cryptic. Hell, I'd do the Chicken Dance and shit out eggs for a cryptic clue right now.

The dead on my porch said nothing. They just stared at me. It was unnerving.

As they began to fade away, Steve stepped forward. For a brief moment, he was back to the wonderful man who I'd spent so many years with. "Daisy," he whispered brokenly. "You have only days to discover the riddle and solve it. Start with the ending you desire and work your way back. It's the only way. Remember nothing is impossible... you just have to believe."

As he shimmered and grew fainter, I spoke up. "Will you be back?"

He smiled. It was filled with sadness. "I will. Though, I'm not really sure why I'm here. Work fast, Daisy. The Light depends on you."

In a gust of icy wind, the dead on my porch disappeared. I turned and looked at Gideon. His expression was unreadable as he stared back at me. My stress felt as if it was eating me alive. Peeling off my skin wouldn't even bother me right now.

"Suggestions?" I asked the Immortals who I trusted with my life.

All I got in response was silence until Lura Belle spoke. "Call me crazy, but I'd start with the Higher Power."

I closed my eyes and wanted to be somewhere else— anywhere else. The best day of my life had taken a seriously messed up turn.

"Bad fuckin' idea," Candy Vargo grunted.

"I'd have to agree," Charlie said tightly.

"You have a better one?" I asked, feeling like I was having an out-of-body experience and watching the scene unfold below.

No one did.

"I'm putting on sweats and tennis shoes," I announced as I marched up the steps to the porch.

"Because?" Heather asked warily.

"Because my dress is fabulous, and I'm not going to mess it up when I kick the Higher Power's ass."

"Ohhhhh shit," Candy Vargo muttered.

I stopped at the front door, turned around and faced my family and friends. "Who's with me?"

Gideon stepped forward immediately, followed by the queens and Candy Vargo. Without hesitation, Heather and my other siblings, along with Tory, Charlie, Tim, Zander and Catriona joined the crew.

"What exactly are we going to fuckin' do?" Candy asked, handing me a toothpick.

I popped it in my mouth and leveled her with a hard gaze. "I have no idea," I admitted. "But I will tell you this, the Higher Power is gonna rue the day it messed with my wedded bliss."

My voice sounded sure and strong. The truth was that I was anything but sure and strong. However, I was going to fake it until I made it. It had worked so far. The Higher Power was in for a surprise. A pissed-off bride who happened to be the Angel of Mercy was about to fuck up Its day, the way It had fucked up mine.

I just hoped I would live to the last chapter of my next adventure in one piece. Midlife had turned out to be a ride, both good and bad. I was leaner and meaner due to my job.

However, I was still me, and I had plans to live in peace, not pieces.

Anything was possible if I believed. I believed. The Higher Power was about to get a lesson in real faith. If the Higher Power thought it was fun to play life and death games with me, It would lose.

All I wanted was to have the time of my midlife, and that was still my plan. Even if it took me until my last breath to get there.

The End... for now.

For the next book in the series, go **HERE!**

NEXT IN THE GOOD TO THE LAST DEATH SERIES

EXCERPT: THE WRITE HOOK

BOOK DESCRIPTION

THE WRITE HOOK

Midlife is full of surprises. Not all of them are working for me.

At forty-two I've had my share of ups and downs. Relatively normal, except when the definition of normal changes... drastically.

NYT Bestselling Romance Author: Check
Amazing besties: Check
Lovely home: Check
Pet cat named Thick Stella who wants to kill me: Check
Wacky Tabacky Dealing Aunt: Check
Cheating husband banging the weather girl on our kitchen table: Check
Nasty Divorce: Oh yes
Characters from my novels coming to life: Umm... yes
Crazy: Possibly

Four months of wallowing in embarrassed depression should

be enough. I'm beginning to realize that no one is who they seem to be, and my life story might be spinning out of my control. It's time to take a shower, put on a bra, and wear something other than sweatpants. Difficult, but doable.

With my friends—real and imaginary—by my side, I need to edit my life before the elusive darkness comes for all of us.

The plot is no longer fiction. It's my reality, and I'm writing a happy ever after no matter what. I just have to find the *write hook*.

CHAPTER 1

"I didn't leave that bowl in the sink," I muttered to no one as I stared in confusion at the blue piece of pottery with milk residue in the bottom. "Wait. Did I?"

Slowly backing away, I ran my hands through my hair that hadn't seen a brush in days—possibly longer—and decided that I wasn't going to think too hard about it. Thinking led to introspective thought, which led to dealing with reality, and that was a no-no.

Reality wasn't my thing right now.

Maybe I'd walked in my sleep, eaten a bowl of cereal, then politely put the bowl in the sink. It was possible.

"That has to be it," I announced, walking out of the kitchen and avoiding all mirrors and any glass where I could catch a glimpse of myself.

It was time to get to work. Sadly, books didn't write themselves.

"I can do this. I have to do this." I sat down at my desk and made sure my posture didn't suck. I was fully aware it would suck in approximately five minutes, but I wanted to start out right. It would be a bad week to throw my back out. "Today, I'll write ten thousand words. They will be coherent. I will not mistakenly or on purpose make a list of the plethora of ways I would like to kill Darren. He's my past. Beheading him is illegal. I'm far better than that. On a more positive note, my imaginary muse will show his ponytailed, obnoxious ass up today, and I won't play Candy Jelly Crush until the words are on the page."

Two hours later...

Zero words. However, I'd done three loads of laundry—sweatpants, t-shirts and underwear—and played Candy Jelly Crush until I didn't have any more lives. As pathetic as I'd become, I hadn't sunk so low as to purchase new lives. That would mean I'd hit rock bottom. Of course, I was precariously close, evidenced by my cussing out of the Jelly Queen for ten minutes, but I didn't pay for lives. I considered it a win.

I'd planned on folding the laundry but decided to vacuum instead. I'd fold the loads by Friday. It was Tuesday. That was reasonable. If they were too wrinkled, I'd simply wash them again. No biggie. After the vacuuming was done, I rearranged my office for thirty minutes. I wasn't sure how to Feng Shui, but after looking it up on my phone, I gave it a half-assed effort.

Glancing around at my handiwork, I nodded. "Much better. If the surroundings are aligned correctly, the words will flow magically. I hope."

Two hours later...

"Mother humper," I grunted as I pushed my monstrosity of a bed from one side of the bedroom to the other. "This weighs a damn ton."

I'd burned all the bedding seven weeks ago. The bonfire had been cathartic. I'd taken pictures as the five hundred thread count sheets had gone up in flame. I'd kept the comforter. I'd paid a fortune for it. It had been thoroughly saged and washed five times. Even though there was no trace of Darren left in the bedroom, I'd been sleeping in my office.

The house was huge, beautiful… and mine—a gorgeously restored Victorian where I'd spent tons of time as a child. It had an enchanted feel to it that I adored. I didn't need such an enormous abode, but I loved the location—the middle of nowhere. The internet was iffy, but I solved that by going into town to the local coffee shop if I had something important to download or send.

Darren, with the wandering pecker, thought he would get a piece of the house. He was wrong. I'd inherited it from my whackadoo grandmother and great-aunt Flip. My parents hadn't always been too keen on me spending so much time with Granny and Aunt Flip growing up, but I adored the two old gals so much they'd relented. Since I spent a lot of time in an imaginary dream world, my mom and dad were delighted when I related to actual people—even if they were left of center.

Granny and Flip made sure the house was in my name only —nontransferable and non-sellable. It was stipulated that I had to pass it to a family member or the Historical Society when I died. Basically, I had life rights. It was as if Granny and Aunt Flip had known I would waste two decades of my life married to a jackhole who couldn't keep his salami in his pants and would need someplace to live. God rest Granny's insane soul. Aunt Flip was still kicking, although I hadn't seen her in a few years.

Aunt Flip put the K in kooky. She'd bought a cottage in the hills about an hour away and grew medicinal marijuana— before it was legal. The old gal was the black sheep of the family and preferred her solitude and her pot to company. She hadn't liked Darren a bit. She and Granny both had worn black to my wedding. Everyone had been appalled—even me—but in the end, it made perfect sense. I had to hand it to the old broads. They'd been smarter than me by a long shot. And the house? It had always been my charmed haven in the storm.

Even though there were four spare bedrooms plus the master suite, I chose my office. It felt safe to me.

Thick Stella preferred my office, and I needed to be around something that had a heartbeat. It didn't matter that Thick Stella was bitchy and swiped at me with her deadly kitty claws every time I passed her. I loved her. The feeling didn't seem mutual, but she hadn't left me for a twenty-three-year-old with silicone breast implants and huge, bright white teeth.

"Thick Stella, do you think Sasha should wear red to her stepmother's funeral?" I asked as I plopped down on my newly Feng Shuied couch and narrowly missed getting gouged by my cat. "Yes or no? Hiss at me if it's a yes. Growl at me if it's a no."

Thick Stella had a go at her privates. She was useless.

"That wasn't an answer." I grabbed my laptop from my desk. Deciding it was too dangerous to sit near my cat, I settled for the love seat. The irony of the piece of furniture I'd chosen didn't escape me.

"I think she should wear red," I told Thick Stella, who didn't give a crap what Sasha wore. "Her stepmother was an asshat, and it would show fabu disrespect."

Typing felt good. Getting lost in a story felt great. I dressed Sasha in a red Prada sheath, then had her behead her ex-husband with a dull butter knife when he and his bimbo showed up unexpectedly to pay their respects at the funeral home. It was a bloodbath. Putting Sasha in red was an excellent move. The blood matched her frock to a T.

Quickly rethinking the necessary murder, I moved the scene of the decapitation to the empty lobby of the funeral home. It would suck if I had to send Sasha to prison. She hadn't banged Damien yet, and everyone was eagerly awaiting the sexy buildup—including me. It was the fourth book in the series, and it was about time they got together. The sexual tension was palpable.

"What in the freaking hell?" I snapped my laptop shut and groaned. "Sasha doesn't have an ex-husband. I can't do this. I've got nothing." Where was my muse hiding? I needed the elusive imaginary idiot if I was going to get any writing done. "Chauncey, dammit, where are you?"

"My God, you're loud, Clementine," a busty, beautiful woman dressed in a deep purple Regency gown said with an eye roll.

She was seated on the couch next to Thick Stella, who barely acknowledged her. My cat attacked strangers and friends. Not today. My fat feline simply glanced over at the intruder and yawned. The cat was a traitor.

Forget the furry betrayer. How in the heck did the woman get into my house—not to mention my office—without me seeing her enter? For a brief moment, I wondered if she'd banged my husband too but pushed the sordid thought out of my head. She looked to be close to thirty—too old for the asshole.

"Who are you?" I demanded, holding my laptop over my head as a weapon.

If I threw it and it shattered, I would be screwed. I couldn't remember the last time I'd backed it up. If I lost the measly, somewhat disjointed fifty thousand words I'd written so far, I'd have to start over. That wouldn't fly with my agent or my publisher.

"Don't be daft," the woman replied. "It's rather unbecoming. May I ask a question?"

"No, you may not," I shot back, trying to place her.

She was clearly a nutjob. The woman was rolling up on thirty but had the vernacular of a seventy-year-old British society matron. She was dressed like she'd walked off the set of a film starring Emma Thompson. Her blonde hair shone to the point of absurdity and was twisted into an elaborate up-do. Wispy tendrils framed her perfectly heart-shaped face. Her sparkling eyes were lavender, enhanced by the over-the-top gown she wore.

Strangely, she was vaguely familiar. I just couldn't remember how I knew her.

"How long has it been since you attended to your hygiene?" she inquired.

Putting my laptop down and picking up a lamp, I eyed her. I didn't care much for the lamp or her question. I had been thinking about Marie Condo-ing my life, and the lamp didn't bring me all that much joy. If it met its demise by use of self-defense, so be it. "I don't see how that's any of your business, lady. What I'd suggest is that you leave. Now. Or else I'll call the police. Breaking and entering is a crime."

She laughed. It sounded like freaking bells. Even though she was either a criminal or certifiable, she was incredibly charming.

"Oh dear," she said, placing her hand delicately on her still heaving, milky-white bosom. "You are so silly. The constable knows quite well that I'm here. He advised me to come."

"The constable?" I asked, wondering how far off her rocker she was.

She nodded coyly. "Most certainly. We're all terribly concerned."

I squinted at her. "About my hygiene?"

"That, amongst other things," she confirmed. "Darling girl, you are not an ace of spades or, heaven forbid, an adventuress. Unless you want to be an ape leader, I'd recommend bathing."

"Are you right in the head?" I asked, wondering where I'd left my damn cell phone. It was probably in the laundry room. I was going to be murdered by a nutjob, and I'd lost my chance to save myself because I'd been playing Candy Jelly Crush. The headline would be horrifying—*Homeless-looking, Hygiene-free Paranormal Romance Author Beheaded by Victorian Psycho.*

If I lived through the next hour, I was deleting the game for good.

"I think it would do wonders for your spirit if you donned a nice tight corset and a clean chemise," she suggested, skillfully ignoring my question. "You must pull yourself together. Your behavior is dicked in the nob."

I sat down and studied her. My about-to-be-murdered radar relaxed a tiny bit, but I kept the lamp clutched tightly in my hand. My gut told me she wasn't going to strangle me. Of course, I could be mistaken, but Purple Gal didn't seem violent —just bizarre. Plus, the lamp was heavy. I could knock her ladylike ass out with one good swing.

How in the heck did I know her? College? Grad School? The grocery store? At forty-two, I'd met a lot of people in my life. Was she with the local community theater troop? I was eighty-six percent sure she wasn't here to off me. However, I'd been wrong about life-altering events before—like not knowing my husband was boffing someone young enough to have been our daughter.

"What language are you speaking?" I spotted a pair of scissors on my desk. If I needed them, it was a quick move to grab them. I'd never actually killed anyone except in fictitious situations, but there was a first time for everything.

Pulling an embroidered lavender hankey from her cleavage, she clutched it and twisted it in her slim fingers. "Clementine, *you* should know."

"I'm at a little disadvantage here," I said, fascinated by the batshit crazy woman who'd broken into my home. "You seem to know my name, but I don't know yours."

And that was when the tears started. Hers. Not mine.

"Such claptrap. How very unkind of you, Clementine," she burst out through her stupidly attractive sobs.

It was ridiculous how good the woman looked while crying. I got all blotchy and red, but not the mystery gal in purple. She grew even more lovely. It wasn't fair. I still had no clue what the hell she was talking about, but on the off chance she might throw a tantrum if I asked more questions, I kept my mouth shut.

And yes, she had a point, but my *hygiene* was none of her damn business. I couldn't quite put my finger on the last time I'd showered. If I had to guess, it was probably in the last five to twelve days. I was on a deadline for a book. To be more precise, I was late for my deadline on a book. I didn't exactly have time for personal sanitation right now.

And speaking of deadlines...

"How about this?" My tone was excessively polite. I almost laughed. The woman had illegally entered my house, and I was behaving like she was a guest. "I'll take a shower later today after I get through a few pivotal chapters. Right now, you should leave so I can work."

"Yes, of course," she replied, absently stroking Fat Stella, who purred. If I'd done that, I would be minus a finger. "It would be dreadfully sad if you were under the hatches."

I nodded. "Right. That would, umm... suck."

The woman in purple smiled. It was radiant, and I would have sworn I heard birds happily chirping. I was losing it.

"Excellent," she said, pulling a small periwinkle velvet bag from her cleavage. I wondered what else she had stored in there and hoped there wasn't a weapon. "I shall leave you with two gold coins. While the Grape Nuts were tasty, I would prefer that you purchase some Lucky Charms. I understand they are magically delicious."

"It was you?" I asked, wildly relieved that I hadn't been sleep eating. I had enough problems at the moment. Gaining weight from midnight dates with cereal wasn't on the to-do list.

"It was," she confirmed, getting to her feet and dropping the coins into my hand. "The consistency was quite different from porridge, but I found it tasty—very crunchy."

"Right... well... thank you for putting the bowl in the sink." Wait. Why the hell was I thanking her? She'd wandered in and eaten my Grape Nuts.

"You are most welcome, Clementine," she said with a disarming smile that lit up her unusual eyes. "It was lovely finally meeting you even if your disheveled outward show is entirely astonishing."

I was reasonably sure I had just been insulted by the cereal lover, but it was presented with excellent manners. However, she did answer a question. We hadn't met. I wasn't sure why she seemed familiar. The fact that she knew my name was alarming.

"Are you a stalker?" I asked before I could stop myself.

I'd had a few over the years. Being a *New York Times* best-selling author was something I was proud of, but it had come with a little baggage here and there. Some people seemed to have difficulty discerning fiction from reality. If I had to guess, I'd say Purple Gal might be one of those people.

I'd only written one Regency novel, and that had been at the beginning of my career, before I'd found my groove in paranormal romance. I was way more comfortable writing about demons and vampires than people dressed in top hats and hoopskirts. Maybe the crazy woman had read my first book. It hadn't done well, and for good reason. It was over-the-top bad. I'd blocked the entire novel out of my mind. Live and learn. It had been my homage to Elizabeth Hoyt well over a decade ago. It had been clear to all that I should leave Regency romance to the masters.

"Don't be a Merry Andrew," the woman chided me. "Your bone box is addled. We must see to it at once. I shall pay a visit again soon."

The only part of her gibberish I understood was that she thought she was coming back. Note to self—change all the locks on the doors. Since it wasn't clear if she was packing heat in her cleavage, I just smiled and nodded.

"Alrighty then…" I was unsure if I should walk her to the door or if she would let herself out. Deciding it would be better to make sure she actually left instead of letting her hide in my pantry to finish off my cereal, I gestured to the door. "Follow me."

Thick Stella growled at me. I was so tempted to flip her off but thought it might earn another lecture from Purple Gal. It was more than enough to be lambasted for my appearance. I didn't need my manners picked apart by someone with a tenuous grip on reality.

My own grip was dubious as it was.

"You might want to reconsider breaking into homes," I said, holding the front door open. "It could end badly—for you."

Part of me couldn't believe that I was trying to help the nutty woman out, but I couldn't seem to stop myself. I kind of liked her.

"I'll keep that in mind," she replied as she sauntered out of my house into the warm spring afternoon. "Remember, Clementine, there is always sunshine after the rain."

As she made her way down the long sunlit, tree-lined drive, she didn't look back. It was disturbingly like watching the end of a period movie where the heroine left her old life behind and walked proudly toward her new and promising future.

Glancing around for a car, I didn't spot one. Had she left it parked on the road so she could make a clean getaway after she'd bludgeoned me? Had I just politely escorted a murderer out of my house?

Had I lost it for real?

Probably.

As she disappeared from sight, I felt the weight of the gold coins still clutched in my hand. Today couldn't get any stranger.

At least, I hoped not.

Opening my fist to examine the coins, I gasped. "What in the heck?"

There was nothing in my hand.

Had I dropped them? Getting down on all fours, I searched. Thick Stella joined me, kind of—more like watched me as I crawled around and wondered if anything that had just happened had actually happened.

"Purple Gal gave me coins to buy Lucky Charms," I told my cat, my search now growing frantic. "You saw her do it. Right? She sat next to you. And you didn't attack her. *Right?*"

Thick Stella simply stared at me. What did I expect? If my cat answered me, I'd have to commit myself. That option might still be on the table. Had I just imagined the entire exchange with the strange woman? Should I call the cops?

"And tell them what?" I asked, standing back up and locking the front door securely. "That a woman in a purple gown broke in and ate my cereal while politely insulting my hygiene? Oh, and she left me two gold coins that disappeared in my hand as soon as she was out of sight? That's not going to work."

I'd call the police if she came back, since I wasn't sure she'd been here at all. She hadn't threatened to harm me. Purple Gal had been charming and well-mannered the entire time she'd badmouthed my cleanliness habits. And to be quite honest, real or not, she'd made a solid point. I could use a shower.

Maybe four months of wallowing in self-pity and only living inside the fictional worlds I created on paper had taken more of a toll than I was aware of. Getting lost in my stories was one of my favorite things to do. It had saved me more than once over the years. It was possible that I'd let it go too far. Hence, the Purple Gal hallucination.

Shit.

First things first. Delete Candy Jelly Crush. Getting rid of the white noise in my life was the first step to… well, the first step to something.

I'd figure it out later.

HIT HERE TO ORDER THE WRITE HOOK!!!!!

ROBYN'S BOOK LIST

(IN CORRECT READING ORDER)

HOT DAMNED SERIES
Fashionably Dead
Fashionably Dead Down Under
Hell on Heels
Fashionably Dead in Diapers
A Fashionably Dead Christmas
Fashionably Hotter Than Hell
Fashionably Dead and Wed
Fashionably Fanged
Fashionably Flawed
A Fashionably Dead Diary
Fashionably Forever After
Fashionably Fabulous
A Fashionable Fiasco
Fashionably Fooled
Fashionably Dead and Loving It
Fashionably Dead and Demonic
The Oh My Gawd Couple
A Fashionable Disaster

GOOD TO THE LAST DEMON SERIES
As the Underworld Turns
The Edge of Evil
The Bold and the Banished
Guiding Blight

GOOD TO THE LAST DEATH SERIES
It's a Wonderful Midlife Crisis
Whose Midlife Crisis Is It Anyway?
A Most Excellent Midlife Crisis
My Midlife Crisis, My Rules
You Light Up My Midlife Crisis
It's A Matter of Midlife and Death
The Facts Of Midlife
It's A Hard Knock Midlife
Run for Your Midlife
It's A Hell of A Midlife
A Leaner Meaner Midlife

MY SO-CALLED MYSTICAL MIDLIFE SERIES
The Write Hook
You May Be Write
All The Write Moves
My Big Fat Hairy Wedding

SHIFT HAPPENS SERIES
Ready to Were
Some Were in Time
No Were To Run
Were Me Out
Were We Belong

MAGIC AND MAYHEM SERIES
Switching Hour
Witch Glitch
A Witch in Time
Magically Delicious
A Tale of Two Witches
Three's A Charm
Switching Witches
You're Broom or Mine?
The Bad Boys of Assjacket
The Newly Witch Game
Witches In Stitches

SEA SHENANIGANS SERIES
Tallulah's Temptation
Ariel's Antics
Misty's Mayhem
Petunia's Pandemonium
Jingle Me Balls

A WYLDE PARANORMAL SERIES
Beauty Loves the Beast

HANDCUFFS AND HAPPILY EVER AFTERS SERIES
How Hard Can it Be?
Size Matters
Cop a Feel

If after reading all the above you are still wanting more adventure and zany fun, read *Pirate Dave and His Randy Adventures*, the romance novel budding novelist Rena helped wicked Evangeline write in *How Hard Can It Be?*

Warning: Pirate Dave Contains Romance Satire, Spoofing, and Pirates with Two Pork Swords.

NOTE FROM THE AUTHOR

If you enjoyed reading *A Leaner Meaner Midlife*, please consider leaving a positive review or rating on the site where you purchased it. Reader reviews help my books continue to be valued by resellers and help new readers make decisions about reading them.

You are the reason I write these stories and I sincerely appreciate each of you!

Many thanks for your support,
~ Robyn Peterman

Want to hear about my new releases?
Visit https://robynpeterman.com/newsletter/ and join my mailing list!

ABOUT ROBYN PETERMAN

Robyn Peterman writes because the people inside her head won't leave her alone until she gives them life on paper. Her addictions include laughing really hard with friends, shoes (the expensive kind), Target, Coke (the drink not the drug LOL) with extra ice in a Yeti cup, bejeweled reading glasses, her kids, her super-hot hubby and collecting stray animals.

A former professional actress with Broadway, film and T.V. credits, she now lives in the South with her family and too many animals to count.

Writing gives her peace and makes her whole, plus having a job where she can work in sweatpants is perfect for her.

Made in United States
Orlando, FL
04 May 2024